IN THE

DARK

OF

WINTER

IN THE
DARK
OF
WINTER

MONIQUE THÉBEAU

In the Dark of Winter

ISBN 978-1-9992078-0-9

Editing and typesetting by Lee Thompson Editing+.
Cover design by Angella Cormier.
Book cover image by Misrad Mujanovic.

Monique Thébeau (publisher)
Riverview New Brunswick Canada
moniquethebeau@gmail.com

For Steve, the love of my life,
and the angels on my shoulder.

CHAPTER ONE (JULY 2002)

*I*N A FIELD NEXT TO AN ABANDONED FARMHOUSE, A SALT-*and-beer-seasoned ninety-pound hog, its flesh spitting and crackling, rotated over an open fire. Word of mouth had brought this crowd together, a no-frill yearly event in the foothills of Blossom Mountain, twenty kilometres south of Moncton. No signage existed and, year after year, the site was only found by come-by-chance, or through the grapevine. This year was no different. The crowd, eager to sink their teeth into the juicy, roast pig, huddled around the farmhouse, whose sagging roof begged for a new spine.*

Early in the evening, Ben Walsh and his wife Maryel drove straight to the party by way of four-wheeler, using backroads and trails. They parked the ATV on Salem Road, behind a thick line of white pines across from the farm. Ben unlatched the tent and sleeping bags from the back of the quad and pitched the tent up, tossing the sleeping bags in it. Then, weighed down by lawn chairs and cooler, they crossed the road and reached the back of the farmhouse.

Ben paused for a moment and stood tall, gazing out at the crowd. The field teemed with hundreds of partiers, their tents, coolers and boom boxes. A roar of laughter and music echoed back as a large wave of new arrivals flooded the pasture. Farther down the field, speakers, resting on mini stages in the sprawling farmland, blared "Magic Bus" by The Who. The drums' rhythm reverberated through his body, pulling him in. He grabbed Maryel's hand and they moved downhill, where the music thumped harder.

For the next hour they moved through the crowd, connecting with old friends, making new ones. And although Maryel's brother, Mike, had insisted on them going to the party, they saw no sign of him.

As the sun set, Ben and Maryel followed a flock of people through a narrow path, crisscrossed with tree roots, that opened up to a gravel pit in the back of the property, closer to a bonfire whose blaze raged against the night. Dozens of people, eyes glowing, sat around the fire, captivated by the flames and its flurry of sparks. The grass was littered with plastic cups and paper plates. In the distance, they heard the beat of ZZ Top's "Sharp Dressed Man."

Ben took Maryel's shoulder and pointed. There was Mike, the only one standing, intoxicated and struggling to keep his balance. The crowd cheered him on as he jumped near the blaze, one minute throwing handfuls of flame-colourant packets, and the next, armloads of deadwood. Mike waved his hands in the air to the beat of "Here for the Party" as if a maestro conducting a Mozart sonata. Girls joined him on the pretend rock stage as the fire strengthened, coughed out flames of blues, green, and hot pink. The inferno intensified, the dancers backed off and the circle of chairs widened.

Ben, nodding to the music, picked a beer can from the cooler. He cracked it open and pushed it down into the mesh cup-holder in Maryel's chair. He fixed himself a Rum and Coke and watched as Mike, normally shy, continued to dance. Ben wished he had a camcorder to embarrass him later.

With the revellers burning through their booze and drugs, straggling and stumbling near the fire, Ben was happy they'd pitched their tent away from the redneck ball. He was cautious. It was their anniversary, after all. Ten years. Ten challenging years parenting Alec, a problem child, but they had stuck together through it all. This party was just what he and Maryel needed to mark the milestone and unwind. Ben winked at Maryel. Her lips quirked at the corners and she shook her head, eyes scanning his chest. She always got a kick out of the T-shirts he wore. Tonight, the white letters *"If found...Please return to the pub"* popped against the black fabric. His long, jet-black hair, tied at the nape of his neck, showed his strong jaw.

Party abandoned and holding hands, they walked past the farmhouse and across Salem Road, retiring to the tent. They undressed quickly and he climbed on top, jostling a bit until he was inside her. She gripped him harder, bracing for climax. He felt her nails on the top of his back go deep; Maryel moaned, shuddered.

Ben woke to the sound of crickets chirping. His dry mouth and the mildew smell inside the canvas tent made crawling outdoors inviting. I should've opened the tent's flaps before heading to the party, he thought. Quietly, he released Maryel from his arms, dressed and slipped out of the tent.

In the dead of night, the full moon shone on Ben as he staggered to a centuries-old pine tree and braced one hand against it, freeing the other to relieve himself. After sitting on the ATV, gazing at the moon, he enjoyed the gentle mid-July breeze on his face. The wind rustled tree-top branches and one could swear it was the sound of a river. A dog barked in the distance and he felt at peace. It was 3:30 a.m. Ben was wide awake now. Whenever he woke up this early, there was no going back to sleep.

He crossed Salem Road and, as he approached the farmhouse's yard of passed-out revelers, he saw the sizzling remains of the unattended hog. He made his way to the fire pit and found a few intoxicated souls debating pointlessly in front of the fire, which was now reduced to sputtering embers.

He turned back toward the farmhouse. As he passed it, he heard an unexpected sound. He cocked his head toward it and listened. A woman's voice. A cry of distress coming from the back of the farmhouse. Quickening his steps, he circled the farmhouse and, unfamiliar with the terrain, slowed his pace but ran when the cries turned to screeching until he reached a window with broken panes. A gas lantern cut through the darkness, illuminating shadows of two tall male figures pawing at a woman pinned down on the floor.

Paralyzed, Ben stood with his jaw tight and knuckles clenched. While his heart raced, readying himself for action, memories of his father molesting his sister Tina flashed through his brain. He turned to find a way in then stopped abruptly when a six-foot-four tattooed man, wearing his scars with pride, pushed the heel of his hand onto Ben's chest. Ben backed off, losing his balance, and when he stabilized himself enough to take a look, he recognized Grinder, his gunmetal eyes and thick neck. Grinder grunted, grabbed Ben and turned him around, making him watch the assault.

"What are you doing?" Ben said, horrified.

"Come on, Ben, look at her!" Grinder said in a penetrating voice. "She's enjoying it… a rebel without a cause. We didn't invite her. She came looking for a good time. Right, Q-Tip?" he shouted through the broken window.

"Jesus! Let go of me!" Ben barked while trying to get out of Grinder's grip.

"You be nice now!" Grinder said, grabbing Ben by the back of neck. "Or I ain't selling you no more dope. Zero, zip."

Ben wanted to say, "I don't need your damn weed," but all he managed to get out was a "Fuck you, Grinder."

Grinder laughed and Ben didn't see the fist coming. Courtesy of Q-Tip, the sucker punch hit his ear, filling his head with spots of light, and he tumbled to the ground. When he scrambled back to his feet, brushing dirt from his cheek, Grinder grabbed his hair and kneed him in the stomach. Ben doubled over, his belly on fire. Grinder pushed him over and he fell on his back. He took a few short breaths, feeling as though there wasn't enough room in his chest for air.

Grinder pulled Ben to his feet. Then, heavy arm over Ben's shoulder, he herded him towards the farmhouse's back entrance. "Let's go say hi!"

Ben slipped out of Grinder's embrace and hobbled ahead of the walrus-moustached biker, the floorboards creaking and dust falling as they stepped through the missing back door and into the occupied room. In front of the broken window, its windowsill weeping scabs of fungus-green paint, a naked girl sat against the wall, chin buried in her chest, hands clamped over her ears, rocking.

One of Grinder's puppets, Rat, sweat pouring down his temples, zipped up his jeans while another one of Grinder's lackeys, Spade, pulled down his dropped-crotch baggy pants.

"This creep was sneaking a peek at the show," Grinder, smirking, told his friends. "Without paying!"

"Didn't take you for a peeping Tom," Rat said, quietly.

Ben crossed his arms and gritted his teeth, all the while keeping his eyes on the young victim. "Didn't know taking a leak was a crime."

Spade lifted the girl off the floor like a rag.

"What are you looking at, moron?" Spade asked Ben as he pushed her back to the floor, pried her legs open, revealing blood. "Never seen a virgin before?" He then fell atop her and Ben, wide-eyed and red in the face, stomped toward them.

"Don't you dare," Grinder boomed, shoving him in a corner of the room, both hands on Ben's chest. "It's true love, can't you see?"

Grinder pointed at Ben to stay put, then led Rock, Q-Tip, and Rat closer to Spade. Grinder, shielding his voice, towered over the three. All Ben heard was the sound of the girl begging Spade to stop. Spade held her arms down and grabbed her face, kissing her. Ben turned away, feeling his chest rise and fall. Grinder motioned for Ben to join them.

"You know what happened to the pig here tonight," Grinder confided, pushing his fingertips into Ben's chest. "Well the same thing will happen to you if you think you're going to save the world of naughty girls. I have a brilliant idea. From now on, you're going to work for me. Move drugs and keep some of my girls from time to time. I hear you got a real nice place back in the woods. Consider yourself lucky that we like you, right boys?"

"Owooooo!" they howled in unison. "We love you man!"

Ben took a deep breath.

"Remember!" Grinder said. "If you don't do what I tell ya, we'll drop this little one dead at your doorstep and call the cops on you, you pervert. Your pad is my pad!" Grinder dropped his smile, lowered his voice. "You know what I can do. Now, get out of my sight."

Ben didn't want to leave, didn't want to leave the poor girl who would be fearful of every man she'd ever meet on the street for the rest of her life. But he did leave. He hightailed over to what was left of the fire, now a bed of embers, and paced, staring into the flames. Then, he picked up a piece of wire, bent the end in a U-shape and kneeled on one knee, stirring the embers absentmindedly until the wire burnt his hand. As the night shadows started to fade, he went to join Maryel in the tent, but he couldn't settle down. He opened the cooler and grabbed a few ice cubes, bringing them to his ear, his hand sticky with blood. "Fuckin' Q-Tip," he thought. Then, he sat on the ground, legs crossed, chain-smoking till dawn.

CHAPTER TWO (2003—)

*A*LL THE SIGNS WERE THERE — LEAVES TURNING, SLOWLY *falling, carrots digging deeper in the ground, seeking moisture, and onions growing skins as thick as leather. In late fall, meteorologists predicted a long and harsh winter and even Joe Lardy, a farmer using slaughtered pigs' spleens to forecast the weather, called for a bad winter. Both were right and Old Man Winter's mayhem would be one nobody in Atlantic Canada would soon forget.*

Jack Thibodeau walked outside and squinted at the sparkling ivory snow, his eyes still full of sleep. A cold breeze had spanked the white stuff against the base of the house, making it curl like the crest of a wave. The street was bare except for a slow-moving garbage truck that stopped squarely in front of his neighbour's trash bin, its hopper swallowing the can's content in one scoop. The compressor's noise echoed loudly as the garbage man, hanging by one arm like a monkey on the back of the truck, now picked up and emptied Jack's trash. A flock of crows flew overhead, black streaks against the dull grey sky as Jack opened one of the garage doors and wheeled the two empty cans to their rightful place. He then wiped the side windows of his truck with a rag soaked in Windex, removing the caked salt and dirt.

After climbing behind the wheel, and with only a few hours of sleep, he, like many generations of transmission-line technicians before him, drove out into the dark of night and listened to the news on the radio:

More than sixty utility poles have snapped like toothpicks in Albert County in the past twenty-four hours. Trees have fallen onto power lines by the hundreds and close to forty thousand homes are in the dark and without power in sub-zero temperatures. In many communities, power may not be restored for several days.

Heading south along Route 114, from Moncton to Alma, he shifted into higher gear. The first explorers had cut the road through rolling hills. Every twist and turn brought with it small pockets of perched homes, their driveways looking more like ski trails, all overlooking the Petitcodiac River, better known to locals as the Chocolate River for the colour of its mudflats at low tide.

The wind howled at the snow pellets, forcing them to veer sideways. Its fury covered the already bleached area with blowing snow. The roads, though heavily salted, were increasingly slippery. Jack inhaled the tepid air of the heater and continued his trek, stopping twice along the way to put homes back on the grid. After a couple of hours, and a third home restored, he jumped into his truck, threw his hardhat on the passenger seat, and poured himself coffee from a Thermos. While the vehicle warmed up, he clutched the cup with his gloves, blowing into it, and brought it to his nostrils. The hot brew's steam curled up from the cup and began melting caked ice from his thick black moustache. With a sweep of the tongue, he licked the melted snow off of his lips.

He drained the cup and wiped the sweat from his forehead with the back of his hand. Holes the size of a Dixie cup emerged on the frozen windshield. He ate a peanut butter and jelly sandwich in two bites and downed it with the rest of the coffee. It was 8:45 a.m. when he dialled home, hopeful that Veronica was up with baby Erica.

He'd first set eyes on her at the library where she worked. In the beginning, he'd slouch in an overstuffed chair on the second level of the library and watch her at a distance.

He'd cover half of his face with a book like a bandit, his eyes not once looking at the pages. What he saw was a boldness that radiated self-confidence and then the hair, black and curly with soft spirals against her olive skin. Perfection! He never withdrew a book when she worked, that was way too embarrassing. One day, he worked up the courage and walked up to the desk to ask her out, but then chickened out. Eventually he succeeded, stuttered out the question, and she said yes.

"Where are you taking me?"

"A movie?"

After the third ring, he heard the recording.

Hi. You've reached Jack, Veronica and Erica Thibodeau. We can't come to the phone...

He hung up and redialled instantly. The phone rang, this time with a mix of static. Someone picked up.

"Hello," a female voice said, and Jack called out, "Veronica?"

"Hello!" the voice repeated. "Hello. Hello."

"It's Jack..." he managed to say before the crackling line went dead. His heart sank to his boots. He wanted to wish his wife Happy Valentine's Day, but Veronica's mother had answered. He was sure of it. Widowed the previous year, she lived in the in-law suite, just as Veronica wanted. Jack worked long hours and having her mom there was a blessing. She'd help Veronica escape boredom and Florence always showed her gratitude by doing her fair share around the house – cleaning, babysitting and cooking dinner.

As the windshield cleared, he absorbed the harsh winter's reality of sagging hydro lines encased in a six-inch sleeve of freezing rain. He put the truck in gear, accelerating slowly. He turned right on Scotsburn Road, the tire chains clunking and gripping the snow-packed, bumpy lane as they moved uphill. He parked along the road, letting the truck run while he chocked the wheels. He climbed the few steps to the bucket and opened the bucket door. Once inside, he pushed the Power Take-Off button and, with his left hand, moved the joystick, raising its boom over thirty feet until it was level with the power lines.

The bucket bounced and swayed against the wind. The buzzing of bright arcing along the transmission lines warned Jack of the danger. Fitted with flexible, rubber gloves, Jack clamped a hot stick onto the line to energize the bucket. Then, he removed the stick, allowing the bucket to remain connected to the line with wired clamps. After that, he wrapped a yellow rubber sleeve around the damaged portion and worked up there for hours, his dexterous fingers focused on ending the blackout and power flashes. When he pushed the lever to come back down, his footprints around the truck were filled and gone.

With the bucket tucked away, Jack tried calling home again, but he couldn't even hear a ring.

He pulled the snow shoes out of the back of the truck, buckled them tight and headed into the bush to check the dangling lines going to the home. The biting wind screamed in the trees and the sleet and snow lashed at his cheeks. Jack barrelled around snapped-down ice-coated boughs while others hung low, thrashed around him. He lumbered over drifts, his snowshoes crunching through the crusty snow, until he finally reached a level area.

A house blinked through the wild white veil. He caught the scent of wood burning. Head down, he trudged over the snow for another twenty yards. There, Jack spotted the silhouette of a house and, moving a bit closer, recognized a log home with an attached carport and a parked black Jeep Wrangler. As he moved closer to the vehicle, he noticed wall-to-wall firewood and heard chimes singing loudly from a corner. Jack then walked pass the Jeep to the far end of the carport where a dark passageway led to the back of the house.

Jack stooped and unlatched the snow shoes before moving into the passageway, letting the cold wind's snap abate. He stood there quietly for a moment of relief, then turned and looked overhead to where the power lines fed into the house. His gaze moved to the house meter-box a few feet away. As he did, something in a nearby window caught his eye. Behind the glass, he saw a man sitting at a table, his back to the window, packaging a white substance into small clear bags. The sight of the man registered in his brain, and he scurried back out and scanned the carport for his snowshoes.

They weren't where he'd left them. He spun quickly, then all light vanished.

CHAPTER THREE

J ACK OPENED HIS EYES TO A DUSKY ROOM. HIS HEAD throbbed. He moved his hand across the lump near his temple, struggling to keep his eyes open. Everything was blurry. He knew he was on his back with a blanket up to his shoulders. He was on a sofa. He closed his eyes again, remembering that he had tried to call home and had been in and out of the bucket before trekking through snow. Had he passed out? Fallen and been rescued? Was he dreaming?

He turned on his side and then slowly sat up, his bare feet brushing against shag carpeting. He stirred his feet in it and it felt comforting. Rubbing his head with both hands, he opened his eyes a little wider. A faint light illuminated his surroundings, and he squinted, making out vague shapes. He was naked.

He sprang up from the worn-out sofa and did a one-eighty. Nothing was familiar.

A female voice echoed behind him: "Are you all right? Take your time. He hit you over the head."

He turned and grabbed a small cushion from the couch, slapping it over his groin as he faced her. A light behind her came on. His nostrils flared at the smell of her perfume and his eyes opened wide at the sight of the blonde now standing in front of him. He unglued his eyes from her and looked around, seeing two more girls sitting at a corner table having something to eat.

Jack held one hand on his head and one on the cushion. "Who are you...where am I?"

Before she had a chance to answer, a door swung open at the end of a long hallway, slamming hard. He startled, angled his head and looked behind the girl. A tall man wearing a goalie's mask painted to look like a skull told the girl to move out of his way. Jack blinked and shook his head, hoping that all of it would go away. But within seconds, Jack was staring at the six-shooter revolver tucked behind the stranger's leather belt.

His face drained of colour as he dropped the pillow and put his hands in the air. "There's no need for that!" The man in the mask grumbled. "Put your hands down. Who are you and why the hell were you on my property?"

Jack crossed his arms to hide his shaking and one of the girls threw him a blanket. "I have the same questions as you do." Without moving a hair, he shifted his eyes back to the blonde, now sitting at a kitchen table with the same two girls seen earlier.

"Jesus, sit down!" the masked newcomer commanded, pushing Jack to the couch. "Sit, I said."

Back on the couch, Jack's mind overflowed. How long had he been here? What was he going to do? How would he escape?

"Who are you?"

"Jack Thibodeau," he answered, his voice wobbly as he stared at the mask. "I'm a lineman for NB Power."

"Right. And you barge into people's homes without knocking?"

It all came back. "I followed the power lines through the woods," Jack blurted out. "I was by the house to check the meter box and get a break from the wind."

"You work for the hydro company!" the stranger said, shaking his head and laughing. "That's great. Thank God you're not a taxman or a cop."

The girls laughed, too. Then the gunman threw Jack his wallet and he caught it, ready to shove his wallet in his pants' back pocket, but quickly remembered his pants were gone.

"Where's my clothes?"

"You won't need them for a while," the man said as he ordered Jack up, pointing him down the hall and into a bedroom.

Jack's voice raised a little as he approached the bedroom. "Okay. What the hell's going on?"

The man grumbled something again, then pushed Jack to the bed where he handcuffed his left wrist to the headboard.

"Come on," Jack said, swallowing deeply. "What have I done to you? I'll leave and promise never to come near your house ever again."

"Just making sure you won't," the stranger said.

Jack watched the man disappear and before he had a chance to piece together what had just happened, the two young girls he'd seen in the kitchen table entered the room and gathered at the foot of the bed.

They bit their lips. "Hey big boy! Want to play?"

"What's this?" Jack barked. "How old are you? You all live here? Tell me, please, what's going on?"

The blonde then swaggered in and, in so many words, told the girls to scram. Wearing nothing but a short, tight black dress, she sat next to him on the bed. He propped his back against the wrought-iron headboard, the handcuffs pulling his right shoulder almost out of joint. She passed him a drink, orange Kool-Aid, and although he didn't want to drink it, the dry devils in his mouth reached out and downed it.

She smiled at him, moved closer and put a reassuring hand on his shoulder.

He jerked her hand away. "Who's the creep?"

"Oh, he's harmless. Just pretends to be tough."

"Who are you?"

She rubbed his leg. "Leah."

Jack shifted his legs away from her, curling them up. "Please, don't."

A creaking sound emanated from the bed as she

moved closer to him.

"Aww… relax. You're safe with me now."

Before long, her voice faded and he floated in mid-air, his eyes losing focus under the bright lights. He lay motionless and in perfect harmony with the world, dreaming of one of the girls going down on him and of their bodies caught up in an erotic rhythm: kissing and holding on to each other, his hands fanning over every inch of her body. He dreamt of making passionate love to Veronica, of lying back in bed exhausted and content, hearing only the sound of their heartbeats.

He woke naked on a soggy mattress with no blanket or handcuffs. He shivered. His throat was dry and there was a bitter taste in his mouth. Reality set in and being awake brought no relief. He tried to stay calm, tried to reason, but none of it made sense. Light spilled under the door, peeling off thin layers of darkness in the room. He jumped up and searched for his clothes by sweeping his feet as he walked around the room. No luck. He got on all fours and patted down the floor around the bed. Still no clothes but after a few minutes, he found his wristwatch under the night table. Veronica had given it to him last Christmas. His hands were clammy as he looked at the time: *10:30 a.m. February 15, 2003.*

He muttered to himself, "Veronica." He'd been here for about twenty-two hours? Who was he dealing with? Would he ever see his family again? He put his watch back on.

With his bladder near bursting, he draped the bed sheet around his body and moved quietly to the bedroom door, opening it just a sliver, his frisson of fear rising with every step. The door flung wide open, missing his face by a hair. Leah threw him a towel.

"Here your go, lover boy," she said as she turned the

bathroom light on across the hall. "Take a shower, you'll feel better."

He blinked against the bright lights in the bathroom and fought a wave of nausea. Grabbing the sink with both hands, he lifted his chin up, looking at himself in the mirror. In it, he saw a man with sunken eyes, pink sclera, and a five-o'clock shadow. Eyes half shut, he discharged his bladder, and the room began to spin. He dropped to his knees and grabbed the toilet bowl with both hands. Within seconds, he retched up the contents of his stomach, mostly bile. Then he turned on the shower and stepped inside, letting the hot water pool in his mouth. He spit the water out and started over, then let the hot water cascade over his head. With the shower stall misty with steam, he relaxed his shoulders, closed his eyes.

He heard a thump on the door and took a deep breath.

"Get out! Now! Where do you think you are? At the Marriott?"

After drying his face, he tightened the towel around his waist, his wet hair dripping down his body. He staggered behind the man's shadow towards the light in the small kitchen. The room looked brighter now and the television played the news. All three girls were sitting around the table. The masked man gestured for him to sit.

"Can I go home now?" Jack begged, his hands wet against his bouncing knees.

Standing next to him, and pointing at the television set, the man said, "Not yet. Have a look at this first, and then we'll talk."

"Can I have my clothes back at least?"

"Nope," he replied. The girls laughed. "You eat first."

"This isn't funny one bit. I don't want to eat. I just want to get the hell out of here."

"I bet you do."

"Milk and sugar?" Leah asked as she poured him a coffee in a thick mug.

"Black," he replied, his foot now bouncing on the floor. He buried his face into the mug, already planning his escape.

She then put a plate in front of him with eggs, bacon and toast and he pushed it away. The man then sat in an office chair, the leather squeaking, and punched a few buttons on the remote control. Jack jumped at the sound of meowing.

On the floor next to him was a banana box full of orange kittens, stirring about in newspaper clippings. He stared at them, clutching the coffee mug with both hands. One of the girls spun up and waltzed over to the television set, inserting a VHS tape into the VCR. The screen turned blue and the stranger laughed. The girls, now sitting next to each other on the couch, chuckled too.

The television screen flickered and then a nude body appeared on the tube, snapping Jack out of his getaway plans. He watched as his hands travelled down a girl's back, down her buttocks and then, turning her around, kissing her neck, her shoulder and her breasts. An immense pressure squeezed his ribs as he glanced over at the couch and made eye contact with Leah. His cheeks flushed.

Jack slapped his hands on the table and pushed himself upright. "You son of a bitch!"

"Sit down," the man said, annoyed. "This is what happens when you snoop in other people's business."

For a moment, Jack was going to protest, but then his whole body began to shake. Angry and humiliated, he stood and paced back and forth within the length of the table like a lion in a four-foot cage. The emotional strike sent him dashing to the bathroom where he slammed the door, furious. Glimpsing at his reflection in the mirror again, he saw himself as he'd never seen before: a desperate man. He folded his hands behind his head and walked in circles, then sat hunched over on the edge of the bathtub. The sound of lovers stopped and footsteps grew closer.

"Well Hydro-Man," the male said flatly after opening the bathroom door and standing in the doorway. "You have a choice. I can either kill you now or we become friends. And I use the word friends loosely, if you get my drift. You keep your mouth shut and you'll never hear from me again, but if you don't, I'll package the movie and send it to your wife. Capisce?"

Jack's mind raced and he couldn't find his voice. All that came out was a slow breath.

"Well?" the voice sparked. "I don't have all day. What's it gonna be?"

"How dare you blackmail me," Jack found himself saying as he stood, trying to make his voice sound stronger. "And not only blackmailing. It's pure bullshit."

"So is that a yes for killing you?"

Jack focused on an empty space in the air between them and answered in a lower voice, "No, I won't say a word. I promise."

"You don't sound too convincing!" the man replied. "The minute you get any bright ideas about our little secret, BANG, someone gets hurt. Understand?"

"Yes!" Jack shouted. "Yes, I do. No one gets hurt."

"Here," the man continued as he threw a bandanna on the floor. "Your clothes are on the bed. Get dressed and cover your eyes."

CHAPTER FOUR

J ACK YANKED THE BLINDFOLD OFF. SHIELDING HIS EYES against the blinding daylight, he sprinted through the snow to his truck hidden under a plaster cast of snow. He keyed the ignition and pushed on the accelerator pedal in a deliberate back and forth motion until the engine roared to life. He blasted the heater and cold air blew in the cabin. He shoved his freezing hands into his insulated gloves, then pulled the ice scraper off the floor and went back outside against his own will, gliding the blade across the frozen windshield. He began hitting it with the tip of the blade, as if stabbing someone. Bits and pieces of the ice, then chunks, flew in the air. He dislodged the wipers and jumped back in the truck, locking the doors.

According to the truck's clock, it was noon. He tried to control his breathing by inhaling short breaths of cold air. He moved closer to the edge of the seat and toggled the windshield washer switch until a few squirts splashed against the window. The wipers screeched behind the glass.

Bringing his cupped hands to his mouth, he blew warm, short breaths to the tips of his fingers. Then he began forcing more windshield fluid out. At last, some of the ice began to disappear and a bit of sunlight bled into the cab. Rubbing his neck in a downward motion, he gulped, hoping not to vomit. Not here. Not now.

Without a hint of hesitation, he changed gears and gunned the truck engine, fish-tailing a few yards before straightening out. Some five hundred meters away, he slammed on the brakes and stopped at the bottom of a hill. He pushed frantically at the side windows' switches. They resisted, then opened grudgingly, inches at a time. Cold air tapped at his cheeks.

He peered out at the glazed surroundings – everything was buried beneath a coat of glittering ice. The trees, fields, and, yes, the power lines sparkled like a million stars as far as the eye could see. He made a left turn and pulled onto Route 114 towards Moncton, sliding over the snowy road until the tires settled in the wheel tracks. He left the windows half open. Ghost birches, immobile behind two inches of ice, bowed out over the road as the truck bounced along. After a few miles, the nightmare sunk deeper.

Accelerating, Jack felt the engine's vibrations in his chest. The desire to throw up choked the adrenaline rush and he pulled over, staggered outside, yellow vomit splattering on his boots. Every breath hurt and he swallowed repeatedly. When the convulsions stopped, Jack gazed at the scenery, appalled at the split tree trunks, twisted branches and broken crowns around him. Thick ice smothered every single tree and shrub along the two-lane suburban road. A dump truck, carrying ten tons of road salt, whizzed by. It was madness. Jack spotted several cars, unattended and barely identifiable, in the ditch. He knocked the snow and vomit off his boots and climbed back in the truck. He turned on the radio:

The vicious snowstorm that pelted southeastern New Brunswick with freezing rain and high winds is finally over. Freezing rain has caused hundreds of trees to fall onto power lines. Utility crews continue to work around the clock to repair broken poles. Most residents in Weldon, Hillsborough and Alma have switched on their lights this morning for the first time since Thursday.

Haunted by the devil on his tail, Jack continued ten more kilometres, his knuckles white behind the wheel as he tried to steer the truck at high speed, barrelling to ninety kilometres an hour in a sixty-kilometre zone as he neared the town of Riverview. More ice-covered trees drooped over houses and power lines, but at least here there were bare spots and slush. He finally downshifted for the light near Gunningsville Bridge. Built in the 1920s, it was narrow and he was prohibited from crossing it with his truck. He'd have to drive another three kilometres through traffic to reach the causeway. He stepped on the gas and zipped through town, shooting across the hundred-meter-wide river in record time. On the other side, roads were snow-clogged with mounds of rutted slush.

At 1:30 p.m., he pulled into the driveway at 123 Old Oak Court, Hazelton Estates, nervous. The large home in the quiet cul-de-sac blended well with the cluster of posh dwellings in the neighbourhood. Lilac shrubs and dogwoods, swollen by the biggest storm of the year, stood like giant snowballs along the walkway to the front door. He brought a handful of fresh snow to his mouth, hoping to mask the foul smell.

Chicklet, their three-year-old Bichon Frisé, plumed tail curved over its back, met him at the door. After taking his gear off, he rushed into the living room where Florence had just finished feeding Erica in her high chair. Florence and Jack gazed at each other and Florence grinned. He got closer, touching his daughter's soft cheeks with the back of his hand. She was sleeping

"Where's Mommy?" Jack asked softly.

"At the gym," his mother-in-law replied. "She's been worried about you. She knows you're on overtime, but she expected a call."

"The gym open today?" he inquired. "And yes, we've been working like crazy. How is she?"

"Restless," she replied without hesitation. "So independent that one... says she wasn't born to change diapers... they make her gag."

"Me too, Florence," he added, forcing a smile.

He then moved to the kitchen and stepped into the

breakfast nook near the bay window. Did Veronica already know? He wouldn't be the first to cheat on his wife, but this wasn't his fault. Shit! She still wouldn't understand. She might not even believe him. He spotted a vase of red roses on the table. Upon closer inspection, he backed up, surprised, before picking up the tag and reading the note again.

Happy Valentine's Day Sweetheart
Can't wait to get home... Jack

His chest tightened and he tried to clear his throat. Hands shaking, he pinned the card back on with difficulty and then shifted about the kitchen, scratching his head. Though he'd already showered, he desperately wanted another. Under the hot water, his mind returned to the hell hole. Who was the damn guy behind the mask? Could I be HIV positive? Should I get checked out?

He stroked the back of his neck, pressing firmly against each cervical vertebra as he reached for a towel. He brushed his teeth, put clean clothes on and returned to the kitchen and stared at the flowers. His daughter's giggling echoed from the living room, but his heart pounded so loud that the baby's cooing could have been miles away.

"I have a roast in the oven," Florence said.

Jack jumped as Florence approached him in the kitchen with Erica in her arms.

"That sounds yummy," he mumbled as he took Erica from her, cuddled her in his arms and slid his pinky into her tiny fingers. "I'm going to lie down for a while, but please tell Veronica to wake me when she gets in."

Looking into his daughter's eyes, he tried to figure out what could possibly happen next. Would the man kidnap his child? Stalk his wife? It was hard to figure out the next move and what he could do about it. He had to calm down and think it through.

"Will do," Florence replied, extending her arms. "You get some sleep."

He kissed Erica's tiny hand and forehead before handing her over. In bed, he slipped under the covers, his back to the door. He couldn't face Veronica. Would she be able to tell? He was too wired to sleep, though, and he spent his time in bed wishing he could go back and change what had happened. Soon a throb in his head forced him to sit and swallow a few Tylenol before laying down again.

"Jack?" Veronica whispered as she entered the room. "Are you awake?"

Rising to his elbow, he spoke up. "Yes. Just woke."

"A long stretch?" she said as she moved closer, holding his head on her chest. "And the flowers, honey, they're gorgeous. Thank you so much."

"You're welcome," he added as he stood to hug her, not wanting to meet her eyes.

"Did you try calling?" she asked quietly. "I answered a call, but it disconnected."

"Bad reception," he replied, rubbing his ear. "I tried several times."

Veronica tightened her arms around him. "It doesn't matter. You're here now and that's all that matters."

He took her hand and raised it to his lips, kissing it in a way that he knew made her heart dance.

Her smile widened, then she stood back. "You're shaking. Is everything okay?"

He kissed her on the cheek. "Tired as hell, that's all."

"Have you slept long?"

"Not long enough..." He hugged her harder. "But I'm staying up."

"Good," she replied as she zipped out of the bedroom. "Hope you're hungry."

He lied. "Starving."

He wanted to hide under a rock, end this new reality. His family was in peril. Nothing could change that, but there was nothing he wouldn't do to keep them safe.

"Another of mom's homemade meals again," she hollered from the hallway.

Jack sat down at the table and, talking fast, filled them in on the events of his absence. He hardly ate, dressed warmly and rushed outside to clean the driveway. Lost in thought behind the snow blower, he decided to turn his home into Fort Knox. While mulling over the fortification, Randy Reardon, a retired Mountie living across the street, waved and sprinted over. Jack stopped, made small talk over the sound of the machine, shook his head every so often, but, more than anything, he contemplated his future. The thought of telling Randy crossed his mind, but not long enough to come out.

"As I've said!" Randy added before heading back to his house. "Let me coach hockey this week. You take a break. You know I'll lose my mind if I don't get out of the house."

"Appreciate that!" Jack replied.

Randy had just closed his front door when a mid-80s decrepit Ford Ranger with rust spots growing around the edge of the door, rattled down the dead-end street. A bicycle lay on top of the snow-bound truck box, its front wheel turning. The truck went to the end of the court, turned around and stopped in front of Jack's house.

This time he shut off the snowblower and stepped backwards on the walkway up to the front door. He heard the truck backfire as he grabbed a shovel, pretending to scrape snow with one hand while twisting nervously at the corners of his moustache. Within seconds, the passenger door flew open and a man jumped into the box and started making snowballs, throwing them a few feet away from Jack. One hit the living room bay window.

He broke into a sweat and his heart was in his throat. Were these the same guys who sent Veronica the flowers? Was one of them the guy blackmailing him? A thousand thoughts clouded his mind as his eyes fixated on the driver, who held a phone to his ear. He shifted his vision to the front of the truck, trying desperately to see a license plate. He was dizzy and bent his head down to take a deep breath.

"Jack!" the voice shouted. "It's for you," Veronica said, swinging the phone in her hand.

He lunged at it and put it to his ear, but all he heard

was a dial tone. When he gazed up at the street again, the truck was gone. Jack wanted to yell or to hide, but Veronica's voice brought him back to reality.

"You've done enough, sweetie. Come inside."

He parked the truck in the garage next to the family van and snow-scooped the large deck and walkway in the back of the house. Then he sat in the living room with Veronica. She pushed her feet onto his lap and he stroked them gently, his eyes glued to reality TV shows until it was time for bed. Veronica fell asleep quickly, but he lay awake for a long time, eventually sneaking out and pacing the house most of the night.

CHAPTER FIVE

BEN GAZED LONG AND HARD AT THE GOALIE MASK before pitching it across the room. It landed on a cinnamon-coloured bearskin rug after bouncing off a cracked wooden statue, as big as life, of a hillbilly smoking a pipe. His chest tightened – it was a curse.

He weaved his hands through his long hair, grabbed at his thick beard, trying to think of happier times, but he couldn't recall any. He didn't know why, but he always plunged from one bad situation into another. This one was the worst.

After the pig roast and, two days later, after Grinder's intrusion of his home, Maryel had stormed out of the house with their eight-year old son, Alec. Alec, deaf-mute and afflicted with cerebral palsy and scoliosis, had been Ben's salvation. And Maryel, the love of his life. As a reputable website designer, she'd survive on her own. She'd telework, meeting deadlines as she always had, often working late into the night while he slept. But he wanted them home with him, to protect them, be a family. He didn't want to become his dad. But it seemed he couldn't do anything right. He wanted to smell the cherry almond scent of her freshly-washed hair and her coconut hand cream again as she hugged him, but he knew she was right. What could he do? Kill Grinder and his gang?

He brooded over his predicament while staring right through Bear, his eleven-year-old sweet-natured Newfoundland. Bear, wagging his tail, looked at Ben with hopeful eyes.

"All right," Ben said, noticing Bear. "Let's go for a walk."

He opened the door and Bear leaped out, racing through the snow for the trees. Within a few minutes he reappeared, tail swirling. Ben picked up a large stick and threw it down a path. Bear barked and lunged, returning it and dropping it at Ben's feet, his brown eyes tugging at Ben's heart.

Bear sprawled on the ground, his paws in front of him, his rear in the air and his mouth open. His nose was covered in snow. Ben tossed the stick yet again and Bear hurtled after it. After a couple more tries, Ben ordered the dog in.

He stepped into Alec's empty room and went to the bed, picking up a stuffed blue velour dragon, its underbelly and wings sparkling with metallic bright gold and purple trimmings. He squeezed its neck and it roared. He brought it to his chest, cuddling it as he closed his eyes. Ben picked up a toy car with a Batmobile look and returned it to the shelf. He moved his eyes to the small white bookcase in the corner and raised a Little Gold Book entitled *Good Night, Little Dragons* to his eyes, running his index finger along its spine. How he wished he could be reading Alec his favourite bedtime story. He sat on the bed.

"Maryel?" he said once he dialled her number. "It's me..."

"What do you want?"

"Just checking in," he replied. "That's all. How's Alec?"

"He's fine," she said coolly. "Just leave us alone."

"I can bring over some of his stuff if you want and we could talk."

"Are they out of your life? Out of our house?" Silence, two seconds, four seconds.

"But, I can still see him, can't I? I miss you guys so much. Please let me spend some time with him. Please. You can take a break this way."

"And get us both killed!" she snapped. "Not a chance.

You got yourself in this mess, you get out of it and then we'll talk."

Click. The phone went dead and he could barely stand the pain in his chest. This time, he retrieved a photo album from his room, where it was locked in his antique steamer trunk. He slumped into a living room chair and skimmed the memory book for pictures of Maryel and Alec. He found a Polaroid capturing their young love's innocence. He was much thinner then, in bell-bottom acid-washed jeans and a tight, open-neck T-shirt. Maryel, pressed against him, wore her thick, curly blonde hair down against an off-the-shoulder top.

He flipped the page, circled his finger around Alec's face when he was a newborn. Then, he flipped to another page and stopped, staring at Alec at five years old. He remembered taking him out after a snowfall, showing him how to make a snow angel. Maryel, from an upstairs window, had taken the shot. It had been months since he had seen his son. He pulled at the corners of the plastic cover until it lifted. He kissed the photograph. Alec had grown considerably since that photo, and he vowed to get them back. He balanced the weight of the album on the tip of his fingers, enjoying temporary freedom from the gang as he fastened the lock back on the strong box.

Ben stoked the fire in the wood stove and stepped outside his log home to the front porch. Around him were stands of old-growth fir, spruce and birch with overhanging branches and missing limbs. He narrowed his eyes against the daylight and put his sunglasses on before jumping on his snowmobile, an antique sleigh in tow. He drove down the ribbon-shaped driveway where, on both sides, branches bowed unwillingly to the ground. On the left, a path led to an old horse-barn.

Wearing only his jeans, hiking boots and a T-shirt, he sagged against the barn door and lit a joint, inhaling each toke slowly. He mused how working in Alaska for many years building radar towers had immunized him to the cold.

Ben touched the rough texture on the door and its tired hinges with his bare hands while looking at the bright, blue sky above, his mind flickering back in time. With a hundred thousand dollars saved from working up north, he had returned home and transformed his mother's transplanted henhouse into a real home. A year later, throat cancer had forced his mother to talk from a mechanical box which she held up to a hole in her neck.

He had tried to start a new life in the house he inherited, not to mention a twelve-acre woodlot in the back yard, but the renovations weren't enough to bury the memories of his mother. Instead, he rented her house and hung his own shingles on the vacant woodlot behind hers, clear out of the view of neighbours.

He took a long drag and dropped the joint, the tip sizzling as it hit the snow. He then opened the creaky barn door: firewood now filled most of the small space, but the barn had once been a refuge.

Ben and his twin brother Tony would collect anything from frogs to grasshoppers and then bring them to their secret place in the barn. Who knew why. Ben studied the white scars of teeth marks on his arm and remembered why Tony had been baptized Gator. He remembered the blood and the pain. Tina, three years older, didn't want anything to do with them. Unless their father was home.

In August of that year, 1971 when Ben was ten, his father, Gerry, resurfaced after having been gone for a week. He had staggered up the weed-filled gravel driveway, a half bottle of whiskey in one hand and his buddy Pete under his arm.

"Get us a glass will you, Rose?" Gerry had said, barging inside to the kitchen table. "Hey kids, come here."

Ben didn't recall all of it, but he remembered his father digging deep into his pockets, grabbing a handful of change and asking Tina to sit on his lap. Walking backwards, Ben and Tony had pulled Tina to the door.

That's when Dad got angry.

"You spoiled brats!" he shouted. "I said, come here, Tina. I am your father and I demand respect."

Nobody moved.

He slammed his fist on the table and, without looking at them, commanded, "Then get the hell away and stay out of my sight!"

Greeted by dark clouds and a sudden down-burst, they scurried under the deep shadow of a large pine tree, gasping for air. Ben still remembered the weakness in his knees and the smell of rain that day. Under the tree, a toad scared the wits out of Tina, and Tony grabbed her hand and led the way down a shaded footpath into the woods, ducking branches until they crossed a stream and found safe haven in the old horse-barn. As the rain rapped on the metal roof, they cursed the old man.

Later that night, when the heavy sprinkle turned into mist, they heard the sound of Johnny Cash coming from the house. When the music and the chatter finally stopped, they sneaked into the boys' room. Ben slept on the floor and let Tina sleep in his bed.

In the wee hours of the morning, loud thumps and sounds of breaking glass came from the kitchen. Startled, the teenagers crawled to the door and peeked from the bedroom as Gerry and Pete fought, chairs and bottles flying. Gerry pushed Pete through the front door and they both fell on the steps and onto the long grass. A storm brewed and lightning flashed the darkness outside. The skies opened up and rain hammered as the two drunk men tried to knock each other out. They used their belts as weapons and the slaps sent chills up young Ben's spine.

After a few minutes, the brawl moved into the backyard. Ben and Tina watched from the back door window while Tony moved to the back steps. Ben remembered Pete and Gerry disappearing into the woods.

"Come on, Ben," Tony shouted. "They might kill each other."

Tina had tried to hold Ben back, pulling on his

shirt, but where Tony went, Ben went. Ben dashed up the trail leading to their hiding place and caught up to Tony. Ahead, the adults were shouting at each other. Ben and Tony followed them at a safe distance and saw Gerry catch up to Pete on the muddy footpath. The sky opened wider, and by the time they reached the barn, the brothers were drenched. Ben remembered dropping to his knees in the mud, his face in his hands, cringing and waiting for it all to end, for the thunder to stop and the shouting to go away. Tony leaped into the fight and, at the next strike of lightning, Ben's wish came true. His father's lifeless body lay motionless with Pete and Tony panting over him.

Half an hour passed before Ben dropped the load of firewood on the tiles in front of the wood stove. Six feet tall and a hundred and eighty-five pounds, he was good looking – straight nose, dark hair and a shy manner that drew women in. No longer a kid, his brown-eyed charm lingered into adulthood. He stroked the scars on his arm.

The smell of firewood and the crisp air used to be enough to relax him. Restless, he stepped outside again and lit another joint, watching as birds – mostly blue jays and grackles – flew around looking for a meal. I should fill the birdfeeders, but who cares, he thought. Let them work for their next meal as much as I do. He made a snow ball and threw it at them.

Ben thought about why he drugged and videotaped the intruder. A precaution, surely, but now he had no choice but to break the news of his uninvited guest before the girls did. He drove to Grinder's workplace– Storky's Waste Remediation Inc. – a front for more than rusted metal, and he had just stepped out of the Jeep when Grinder hustled over to him. Ben told Grinder about the incident and Grinder called him every unchristian name in the book. After Grinder calmed down, Ben told him about the video tape and how he had blackmailed the guy.

"What do you know," Grinder said in amazement. "Didn't take you for being that smart. And you're here to give me the tape?"

"It's well hidden," Ben replied quickly.

Grinder blew snot in a tissue. "I want the tape, Ben. Now."

"Calm down. I'll give it to Mouse when I see him."

"No way. I want it in my own hands."

"Don't trust your puppet?"

"Get out of my face," Grinder replied, chucking the spoiled tissue in Ben's car before walking off.

A smile of satisfaction rose to his lips and Ben couldn't keep the goofy grin off his face as he strolled back into his house later on. He had the tape and there was no way they were getting their hands on it.

The phone rang. He crushed his cigarette in the ashtray and picked up the receiver.

"Hello."

"Happy Birthday, Ben," Tony said with excitement.

Ben was pleasantly surprised. "You're late...and Happy Birthday to you, too, Gator. We need to talk. Soon."

"Just say when."

"Come down tomorrow night and book a room at the Fox, where we used to party in the old days," he said. "I'll be there at 5 p.m."

"You bet," Tony replied. "I'll bring beer and you bring you know what."

CHAPTER SIX

VERONICA SAT BEHIND THE WHEEL AND REACHED over, squeezing Jack's hand for a few seconds. "You know I adore you."

"And I love you more," he replied, holding her hand between his. "Thanks for driving. I could get used to you being my chauffeur."

"You're sitting there because you're the babysitter. One cry from the back and your shift starts."

He took the camera out of its case, knowing the exact spot where she'd stop on the way to his parents' house in Shediac. It was an annual trip, a day when just the right temperature brought out both the anglers and the fish. Veronica stopped before crossing the bridge into the coastal town, pulling over to the side of the road in plain view of the fishing shacks on Shediac Bay. She rolled the window down and Jack handed her the camera. The lens zoomed at the clusters of portable huts dotting the harbour. It didn't compare to the glamour of yachts and sailboats seen during the summer months, but she loved them just the same. She climbed out of the van and leaned her back against the driver's door.

"I see generators next to some of the shacks? They carry all that gear over on the ice?"

"The generators are for lights and they bring everything on a truck. Most of those cabins have two ski-runners on the bottom anyway, ready to be scooped away if temperatures climb too high. I've seen some stuck in the ice after a thaw, and I've even seen some shacks abandoned in the spring and we'd bet on which day they'd tip in."

"You know you have no life when..."

She continued taking pictures of the huts as they stood fearless against the wind, their stove pipes coughing plumes of smoke.

"There's even a travel trailer in the bunch... Huh, I can see the wheels underneath. They never cease to amaze me," she said as she climbed back into the van.

Jack laughed. "If you want to go ice fishing, I can arrange it," he said.

"Thanks," she replied. "But, no thanks. I'm fine looking at them from here."

Jack shrugged. Veronica took the camera strap from around her neck and slid the camera back into its case. She rubbed her hand behind his neck and rolled her window back up, looking at him.

Jack looked at her, surprised. "What?"

"You sure you're okay? That's the most you've spoken to me all week."

"It's winter. You know I get tired this time of year. Just long hours in the cold, that's all. See, I slept in this morning and I'm feeling great now."

"You'd tell me, though, if something was bothering you, right?"

"Absolutely," he answered, the corners of his mouth turning up.

The last thing he wanted to do was spend a Sunday afternoon at his parents but being too tired or stressed out was no excuse. His parents would be flying south for a few months next week, and they wanted to see all of their kids and grandkids before the trip. Who knew, it might cheer him up, perhaps even lower the constant vibration of anxiety in the back of his mind.

His parents were happy to see them. His mother took Erica in her arms as soon as they set foot inside. They promised to send pictures and call while they were away.

On the way home, Jack was more relaxed, having laughed enough to store for a while.

Home, he clipped Chicklet to her leash and came through the back door humming, but his mind-chatter exploded when he saw the Valentine's flowers again.

"I'm taking Erica in for a diaper change," Veronica said from the hallway. "We should call for pizza. What do you think? Ask Mom if she wants anything."

"You okay with donairs? I know how your mom loves them."

"Sounds good to me."

After dinner, while standing in front of the living room window, lost in thought, Veronica called out to him, jarring him from his reverie.

"Is Chicklet with you Jack?" she asked.

"No," he replied. "I thought she was with you."

Jack rushed to the back door to let Chicklet in, but there was no sign of her. He pulled at the leash and found nothing at the other end. This angered him. He stormed out of the house, knocking on each of the twelve front doors on his street. When he returned half an hour later, he'd given up all hope of ever finding her. Under the motion-sensor lights that illuminated the property, he scanned the area, trying to find prints. There were none.

"You know how she loves people and attention," Veronica said. "Anybody could have picked her up."

"What?" he said, shaking his head. "Someone kidnapped her? Why?"

"I don't know why, but where is she?" Veronica asked, stroking his cheek softly with her open hand. "Let's get Mom to look after Erica while we both go look for her."

Once outside, they took turns calling Chicklet's name as they walked the cul-de-sac and adjacent streets. Jack wanted to believe her, and to forget the past week altogether, but he knew this was no coincidence. Who in their right mind would steal a dog in the dead of winter on a back deck? He was annoyed by it and his mind started racing again.

They returned home empty-handed.

He joined Veronica in bed, but once she fell asleep, he got up quietly and sat on the sofa. Jack's thoughts crept into shadowy corners. No doubt Chicklet was taken. No doubt *he* took her. Unable to control his rampaging anxiety, Jack didn't fall asleep until the early hours of the morning.

"What are you doing up so early?" he asked Florence as, eyes heavy with sleep, he stepped into the kitchen.

"I found a picture of Chicklet," she replied, waving the picture in her hand. "If we don't find her soon I'll put a few posters out."

Swallowing his frustrations, he jumped in the shower, washed quickly, dressed and geared up for another work day. He opened the truck door and slid across the seat. His stomach dropped at the sight of Chicklet's blood-soaked white fur lying on the floor mat on the passenger side.

He couldn't bring himself to take Chicklet's body inside. They'd be devastated. Worst yet, they'd want to call the cops. His knees weakened. He pulled himself together, climbed out of the vehicle and went back inside, grabbing a few garbage bags – black ones – and shoving them into his coat pocket.

He drove off, staring at the road ahead for ten long minutes before stopping on the northeast side of the city on Irishtown Road. He parked behind a small white clapboard church and stepped out of the truck, scanning for people.

He put his gloves on and slid his hands under the mat holding Chicklet, which revealed the deep slice running across her throat. He walked over to the highest snow bank behind the church property and climbed it. He stood on top of the bank and pulled a garbage bag from his left pocket, swinging it open in mid-air and slipping Chicklet inside with his right hand. He closed the bag tight and then double-bagged it. He then swung and threw the bag as far as he could. He scrubbed the mat with snow before setting it back inside the cab.

On his way back to town, he noticed a sign along the road: *Atlantic Alarm & Sound*.

A few minutes later he walked up to a payphone and scanned through the yellow pages.

Chuck Hanley was driving south on St. George Street in a brand-new Ford Explorer which he had bought knowing it would be his last car before retirement. He slowed, then parked in front of Arthur Gautreau's shop. The word *Pawn*, in large, bold capital letters on a yellow canvas, beamed above the bay windows, whose glass was covered in more writing – *We buy anything of value – We pay more than anywhere else*. He knew the owner well. He'd been there many times when he worked for the Special Crime Unit.

"You called," Chuck said, nodding to the owner while placing his hat on the counter.

"I may have found you a pearl," he replied. "Come look at this."

They walked to a glass counter and Arthur reached from under the glass, pulling out a Canon. At that exact moment, Chuck's cellular phone rang. He scrambled to get his phone out of his pocket.

He combed his short hair with one hand and pulled his glasses down to the tip of his nose with his other hand, squinting to see the caller ID. He despised those Unknown Name, Unknown Numbers, but business was business and making a buck was the name of the game.

"Hello," he said after pushing the phone button with his pudgy fingers.

"Is this Hanley's Investigations?"

"The one and only," he replied with enthusiasm. "How can I help you?"

"Can I talk to you in private?" the caller asked, and without giving Chuck a chance to answer, continued, "Are you available today?"

"Sure," Chuck said. "Meet me at noon at Keddy's on Shediac Road. That's where I break for lunch. I wear an Indiana Jones hat. You can't miss me."

"Great," said the caller. "I'll see you at noon... Name's Jack."

After a law enforcement career spanning several decades and then a boring retirement year, Chuck had opened a private investigator's office. Business boomed with a full-time secretary, a few security guards sifting through the malls for shoplifters, and two agents. A mountain of fraud and adultery suspicion papers filled his newly-renovated office space. Paula Sears didn't only answer phones, she could pull gags to obtain confidential information. Matt King and Sarah Long – she was nicknamed *Bloodhound* – both in their thirties, handled mostly matrimonial surveillance and there was no lack of work for both of them.

Chuck had strong eyebrows, though his nose was warped by his passion for playing hockey. He was fit for his age and burnt a lot of calories at the gym daily so that he could eat as he pleased, but winter months were especially tough and he struggled to keep the weight off. Sure, he had promised himself to watch his thickening waistline on New Year's Day, but jumping from one diet to another only made him bitter and could only be fixed with a good dose of Fettuccine Alfredo.

Fifty-eight-year old Chuck, with his thick salt-and-pepper moustache, walked out of the camera shop proud, holding a rarely-used Canon Power Shot G2 digital camera. He wrapped the package under his arm and hurried his vehicle to the office, eager to show off his new toy. No one, however, was there, so he puttered around the office until he drove to meet his client. He might be dealing with a jealous man, desperate to find his wife cheating. Maybe he could use the camera right away. When he opened the hotel's front door and stepped into the lobby, he identified his client instantly – the one agitated, pacing the floor. The client spotted Chuck's hat.

"Hanley?" asked the stranger as he moved closer. "Do you have a business card?"

Chuck pulled a card out of his wallet.

"I'm Jack," he said, holding the card up to his eyes. "Just Jack for now."

They sat facing each other at a corner table in the back of the restaurant. Chuck watched as Jack took his sunglasses off, his instincts picking up on the fear in Jack's eyes.

"Just coffee for me," Jack ordered without looking at the waitress.

"The special as usual, please. What is it today?"

"It's meatloaf," said the waitress, her hands on her hips.

"That sounds great!" Chuck replied, his mouth watering like a spring. "And a side of gravy, please."

"Anything to drink with that, sir?"

"Coke," he added. "Please and thank you."

Minutes later, Chuck sunk his teeth into his lunch while Jack fed him the chain of events, from being taken hostage, to ending up in porn, to how flowers were delivered to his wife without his knowledge. He could feel a sense of relief leaving his client's body.

"Ever see him around?" Chuck probed as he dipped his finger into the gravy.

"No," Jack replied, annoyed. "I already told you, he wore a goddamn goalie mask the whole time I was there. It was shaped like a skeleton face in red, black and white, like the one worn by Gary Bromley when he played for the Canucks."

Between bites of meatloaf and making constant eye contact with Jack, Chuck also heard about the dog and how he disposed of it a few hours earlier.

"Oh," Jack blurted out. "Before I forget, somebody

drove up my street Friday night when I was cleaning my driveway. A Ford Ranger, an old beater, more like a rust bucket... kind of a beige colour. Probably mid-eighties. There was a bike in the box on top of the snow. They drove to the end of my street, turned around and drove back to the front on my house, stopped at the end of the driveway and one of them threw snowballs at the house. They were laughing. I took the license plate... *GEN- 477*. Can you find it and get back to me?"

Chuck started at Jack. "Don't you think you should go to the cops with your story?"

"You don't understand," Jack replied in a panicked voice. "He told me he would send the video to my wife if I went to the cops. And Christ, he killed my dog. Are you for real?"

Chuck put his head down and wrote the plate number in his notepad. Jack started to get up, but Chuck waved him down. His experience had taught him a few things besides reading people's physique. He leaned closer to him.

"What's your last name and address?"

"Why do you need that?" Jack asked in a tone that could have frozen water.

"Don't you want me to check out the Ranger you saw?" Chuck asked. "Isn't it there, at home, where you saw it?"

"Yes," he replied. "Uh-huh... Okay, but don't you show up at my house. 123 Old Oak Court off Mountain Road and my last name is Thibodeau."

"For all you know, the guys you saw on your street may have families or friends who live on your street," he added. "May have nothing to do with you."

Jack neither moved nor answered. He simply stared at the table, unblinking.

"And where were you held captive? Do you have an address?"

"Scotsburn Road off of the 114," Jack replied. "I think it's number 133, but not a hundred percent sure. Remember spotting it on the mailbox on the way out but was not in the mood to log it in my book. It's about a quarter of a mile in on the left. I know you can't see the house from the road."

Hanley clicked his pen twice before touching the nib of the pen close to his notepad while looking at Jack. "Aren't you going to ask me how much I charge?"

Jack shrugged. "Sure."

"Fifty an hour," Chuck said without skipping a beat.

"No problem. What's next?"

"Let me find out what I can on that truck and I'll call you," he said. "Where do I call?"

"Call my cell," he replied as he wrote down the number.

Jack worked the rest of the day, flinching at noises and trying to quiet the voices, full of rage, in his head. He arrived home at 6 p.m. Florence and Veronica were sitting long-faced at the table and, when the phone rang, they both jumped. Jack grabbed it quickly.

"You going to the hockey game tonight?" Randy asked.

"No," Jack replied. "I'll pass."

"No worries. Just checking in."

He hung up and he tried to focus. Veronica and Florence wanted answers, but he didn't have any.

"Damn Randy."

Veronica shot up and stood in front of him. "What's wrong?"

"He was over here the other night and told me not to worry about hockey practices, but then every game he calls here to know if I'm going. He's getting on my nerves."

"Bad day? He's always been like that, Jack. As soon as he sees you pull into the driveway, it's like a light goes off and he has to call."

Jack grimaced while making a beeline for the fridge. "Well," Jack said, turning toward her, "I'm getting sick of it."

"The ad will be in tomorrow's paper," Florence said to take the tension away. "You'll see, someone will find her and bring her back.

"Thank you, Mom," Veronica said.

"By the way," Jack said. "I called to book an appointment to have the house burglar-proofed."

Florence changed the water in the bouquet.

"Really? Why?" asked Veronica.

"It's just..." Jack hesitated, felt a lump form in his throat as he glanced at the flowers. He rubbed his moustache. "It's just, a guy from work had his home broken into and he convinced me to take some precautions."

"You're fidgeting," Veronica said as she approached Jack. "What aren't you telling me?"

There was silence.

Jack shrugged. "You can never be cautious enough, that's all," he said quietly. "Come on, don't make a big deal about it. Just playing safe."

CHAPTER SEVEN

A T 8 P.M., Sunday night, Ben knocked at hotel door number 2. A man opened. His hair looked like a field of wheat expertly cut by a sharp scythe, but the rest of his face was identical to Ben's own, including his eyes, the colour of brownies. The man threw his arms around Ben until he couldn't breathe anymore.

"Let go of me, you big thug!" Ben said, trying to squeeze himself out of his grip.

Tony grinned. "I'm just glad to see you, Ben."

They exchanged good-natured insults and settled in and reminisced about the old times, shifting to Tony's years in the army and Ben's run-ins with Grinder and his crew. Then they talked about Tina, and Ben recounted how often he had tried to spend time with her, but she was always too busy.

Ben started rolling a joint. "The last time I saw her, I gave her some pot. She sounded maybe a bit excited, but still real dull."

"Yeah, she's always been too quiet," Tony said. "And on edge."

"Well, I mean, after all she'd been through with Dad, do you blame her?" Ben asked.

Tony shrugged, waved Ben's question away. "Don't know about that. Stuck up, is what I think. Was she ever even close to Mom?" Tony asked. "You know, after I left?"

"Wanted nothing to do with Mom," Ben replied. "I think she's always blamed Mom for not protecting her and never really had any friends. Except for a girl in school who got her a job at the grocery store. She stayed with the girl's family for a long time and even the family wouldn't go near Mom."

Tony took the joint from Ben. "Right fucked up bunch we are," he said, exhaling.

It was two o'clock when they shut the lights off. Ben lay under the covers, happy to have his brother back, but unsure whether to trust him. He never trusted Tony, especially when he was being agreeable. He had seen that mean streak too many times.

When the sun began peeking through the curtains in the morning, the twins woke and, within minutes, began chitchatting again. At ten o'clock, they left the Fox and stepped out into the cold and walked across the street to Mugg's for breakfast. The tone turned as Ben told him about Jack Thibodeau and the misfits.

"You have those assholes breathing down your neck?" Tony questioned, upset.

"What would you do? Go to the cops? We could tell them about what happened years ago, too. That was self-defense, right?"

"Dig up that nightmare!" Tony whispered. "What's wrong with you? Have you lost it? No way are you dragging me into that!" Tony rubbed his jaw. "You ever hear about Pete?"

"Nope. Never saw him again."

"Remember the old bastard? Remember how he locked us up in the trunk of the old beat up '59 Impala in the yard?"

Ben didn't want to remember how scorching it had been that day in Grade One when they jumped off of the school bus and found their father, and Pete, and even their mother intoxicated at the kitchen table. When Tony put his school bag on the table and upset Pete's drink by mistake, the old wino picked them both up by the back of the collar and dragged them to the Impala, throwing them in the trunk and closing the lid. What seemed like hours later, Tina ripped the back seat of the car with scissors to free them.

"The old fucker!" Ben added. "He was worse than the ol' man."

"You were too slow, Ben. He didn't catch me too many times, but I guess that means he caught you. But why would you want to dig that up?" Tony paused for a moment. "No one ever came looking for Dad, eh?"

Ben squirmed in his seat and shook his head. "Not that I'm aware of. I remember thinking the cops would be all over the place after Mom filed the missing person report. But I don't think anyone cared."

"If that was today, I tell you, somebody would be doing something about that. But Dad doesn't deserve a dignified funeral. Let him rot in that hell hole!"

"Yeah, let him burn..." Ben nervously tapped his fingers on the table. "Listen, what about the Storky's?"

Tony grinned too widely. "Where do Grinder and his gang hang out?"

Ben thought he saw a spark in his brother's eye. "Mostly at their camp, The Trap, on Glen Frost Road, or at the Swamp Donkey pub by the airport."

"A new pub?"

"It's the old Foundry pub. New owners."

Tony nodded. "I want you to forget about *we*. There is no *we*, in *we* are doing something. You're on your own man. *And.* For beginners, leave the cops out of it. You think you're in trouble now?"

Ben looked out the window. "I don't know how to get out of it."

"Okay," his brother said, feigning a long sigh. "Give me some time. I'll call you next week."

"Why can't *I* call you? Why don't you ever give me your freakin' number?"

"What about those cuties in your basement, Ben?" Tony asked, chuckling. "Are they pretty? Are you being a bad boy?"

"Gator," Ben said, giving him the bird with his right hand, "I wouldn't touch that filth with a ten-foot pole."

"Ever tell you that Spade worked in a topless bar near our military base a few years back?" Tony asked. "Worked as a handyman at the bar for about a month. At least that's how long I'd seen him there. Every time I'd see him though, he'd turn away from me. I even tried talking to him, but it's like I wasn't even there. Totally ignored me. I should've known. One day, some of our shit was stolen. Pistols, hand grenades, three fucking antitank rockets... stolen right under our nose. And Mr. Spade after that? Long gone. Coincidence? Doubt it. Watch yourself," he added, making his hand into a pistol and pointing slowly at Ben's chest. "Bang."

Ben left shortly after, imagining that it had always been like this, that they'd been normal brothers and that they'd always been there for each other. Relieved and full of confidence, he pulled up next to Grinder as the big man stepped out of his truck at work. Grinder's jaw dropped.

"What do you want?"

"When are the girls moving?"

Grinder kicked the door of Ben's Jeep. "Today... after dark. And don't you dare come around here again, you hear me?"

"*Easy* now!" Ben exclaimed. "What time?"

Grinder spun and walked away. "Midnight sharp!"

Monday night rolled around and Ben dozed off on the couch, watching TV. The phone's ring woke him. It was 11:50 p.m.

"Everything ready to go at midnight?" asked the voice at the other end.

"You betcha," Ben muttered. The phone went dead.

He opened the solid beech cupboard above the fridge

and reached for a bottle of whiskey, pouring himself a drink, straight. He then sniffed a few pieces of day-old pizza, took a bite and chewed the rest as he bounced downstairs and ordered the girls upstairs. The girls, half asleep, stood in the open living room heavy with travel totes clutched to their bodies. He was sitting on the couch when he heard a banging that didn't pause and clearly would not stop until the door was open. Spade walked in and when he left seven tired girls trailed behind him, bulging suitcases in hand, into the back of Grinder's black, tinted-window SUV.

Ben pulled the red, half-empty pack of du Maurier King cigarettes out of his shirt pocket. He opened it and swiped it under his nose, smelling the sweet aroma of dry tobacco before lighting one up. He finished his smoke and his shoulders began to settle back down.

When dawn broke on Tuesday, February 18, Ben got up and toured the basement for leftover residue. He vacuumed and dusted everything, bleached the bathroom and changed the bedclothes before stepping foot outside at dawn.

He breathed in the crisp winter air, pulled the tarp off the snowmobile. Sitting, he pulled the cord and grabbed the handlebars. He revved it twice, then was off, its skis making a right turn on Scotsburn Road and then another right on Creek Road. He drove by Downey's Mill, down a steep hill surrounded by red spruce, red maple and yellow birch, then under a train trestle and veered to the right on the fork in the road. He didn't have to ride this back way. It would've been quicker to just take a left turn coming out of his driveway and go up Scotsburn Road, but the scenery was too pretty to miss. A few miles farther, he turned in Adam Reef's yard next to the oil fields and beached his sled. He opened the oversized garage door and smiled at his babe – a red, blue and yellow twenty-and-a-half-feet long Chinook recreational monoplane. He checked the rudder, the aileron and throttle cable casings, making sure they were coated with WD40 before getting into the narrow cockpit.

He squeezed the bulb to fill the carburetor float bowls with gas, pulled the choke and turned it until the engine fired. He then turned the choke off and let it warm up. Cold as it was, it would take at least eight minutes before it was ready. While waiting, he set up the GPS in a soft bean-pouch glued to the dash and strapped the dual-shoulder harness across his body. At the very last minute he put on the cheap, second-hand helmet. He'd take it off in flight; it was too warm, but during takeoff it was a necessary nuisance.

He eased out of the metal hanger and parked the sport craft momentarily to close and lock the garage door. He shut the tiny cockpit and crossed Dawson Road before taxiing down Stevescote Road, a perfect airstrip since the three-mile road was kept open in the winter for its only occupant, who lived at the very end of the road. The house belonged to Virgil Skead, a Second World War veteran. Ben knew him and always called him ahead of his flights as a precaution.

Ben was pushed gently back in his seat as the aircraft accelerated and gained speed along the snow-packed road. Then the nose of the plane rose and he saw the ground move away. After a minute or so, the vet, who always came out when Ben flew by, stood outside his front door waving.

Once airborne, he kept pulling up the nose and taking altitude. The sky was clear and he peeked down at Route 114 and then at a few cross-country skiers with their long and narrow skis on a wooded trail. The Gang had stolen a piece of his life, but up here they couldn't touch him. He pushed higher and drifted effortlessly over White Rock Hills, the dykes, Sawmill Creek's covered bridge, Caledonia Mountain and over Mary's Point, Dennis Beach and Cape Enrage. Around noon, he flew over Shepody Mountain and circled around Riverside-Albert, landing the aircraft on a deserted Mary's Point road. He lit a joint and sipped on a beer, listening to the peacefulness of the crisp breeze blowing on his face. The wilderness comforted him.

He closed the cockpit up and hit the right rudder to rotate the airplane, pointing towards home. He stared in awe as the sky filled with stars. Below, the city lights sparkled in the distance. As he approached the runway on Stevescote Road, he went into a slip, bleeding off speed, slowly letting it down, down, down until its skis touched the ground.

Early Tuesday morning, Chuck tiptoed out of the bedroom and after twenty quiet minutes of making coffee and showering downstairs, he took the car keys from the hook and hurried out the door. Under snowfall, he shot out of town and found Scotsburn Road.

Once there, Chuck looked right and left until he realized that number 133 would be to his left, but he didn't find it. He continued driving up a long hill heading west, counting five houses along the way on the right and four on the left. When he reached the top of the hill at the end of the road, a rusted metal gate greeted him. Since the gate was open, he drove in. He steered his vehicle around the abandoned oil fields' frosted roads for a short distance and coasted back down Scotsburn Road. He slowed his vehicle, watching the left side closely, and about a quarter of a mile from Route 114 a small home appeared in plain view with several sheds tucked behind it. Next to it, he saw a driveway, which disappeared after a short distance behind a woodlot.

He turned in the driveway, finally saw number 133 on the mailbox, and followed the driveway's curves up to a log home. A Jeep sat in the yard, next to a massive sleigh. Snowmobile tracks were clearly visible around the vehicle. The chimney spit out smoke, and when he knocked on the door a dog barked, but nobody answered. He wrote down the Jeep's license plate number in his notepad and drove back to town.

He returned home and pulled out a thick slab of ham from the fridge, a fresh bun, and mustard. The corners of his jaw ached in anticipation. At the table he picked it up with both hands and sank his teeth in, satisfying his hunger.

He then went back on the road, eyes scanning, coasting for a beige mid-80s Ford Ranger. After sweeping city streets visually, following the dirty caps of snow banks, he headed outside town and up Airport Road. He had a hunch.

He spotted the Ford truck sitting at the Swamp Donkey. He parked across the pub in a long-haul trucker's yard and propped the hood open, the camera hanging from his neck. Above the motor, he aimed, zoomed and snapped pictures of anyone arriving or leaving the pub. A truck with the inscription *Sheppard's Transmission* arrived and he bowed his body even deeper under the hood.

When all worthwhile activity stopped, Chuck left, but he didn't go back to work right away. He parked near the city waterfront and strolled through the snow-packed walking trails of Bore Park until he stood at the edge of an observation deck along the Petitcodiac River. The river was at low tide. Chuck, motionless, stayed long enough to see the tide roll in and the brown river reverse, swell, and wash away the ice-laden banks.

A noisy cloud of seagulls followed the tide. Chuck took a long breath, letting the cool, fresh air not only revitalize his lungs but also his spirit.

An hour later, back at the office, Chuck sat, thinking back over the last few days. Yeah, a bit strange to have a lineman kidnapped for snooping in a window. Then drugged to make porn and use it as blackmail. And who'd slash a little dog's neck? He'd seen his share of sickos, sure, but this case... He shook his head; he needed a drink. When he left for home, the sun was starting to dip, peeking behind the clouds like an eyeball behind drooping eyelids.

He parked the Explorer in the garage, shut off the ignition and walked in to an empty house, realizing that Sharon had gone next door to play cards. He read the note left on the kitchen table.

Your supper is in the fridge
Love xoxo

He jumped in the shower, changed into his tattered gym pants and, with Ben's Jeep's license plate number in hand, called Jack, but there was no answer. Well, it could wait until tomorrow. A drink, though, that couldn't wait. He went to the liquor cabinet and opened a bottle of Johnnie Walker's red label Scotch whisky. He took a slug straight from the bottle and then poured some in a glass. Ice clinked gently in the glass as he rolled it absently between his hands. This Thibodeau case was such a strange one. Thoughts of the kidnapper's goalie mask came into his mind, which led Chuck to reach for the remote control. Hockey. Leafs versus Bruins. The first period had just ended when Sharon walked in.

Sharon hung her coat in the closet and crossed the room to sit in an armchair. "Hey, hon."

Chuck reclined further in his Lazy Boy and smiled at her. "How you doing? How'd cards go?"

"Had some good laughs and I even won a few games. Made four bucks and twenty-five cents. You know it's my last shift this week," Sharon said with relief. "I only go back on the twenty-second. What do you say we get away for a couple of days?"

Sharon, a registered nurse, worked part-time at the City Hospital. Her long blonde hair and even longer legs had him hooked in 1966 when they bumped into each other in the hallway at the hospital. He had picked her up for their first date in his 1965 Ford Mustang with the likes of "I got You Babe" from Sonny & Cher blaring on the eight track player. They were married a year later and a model Ford Mustang sat proudly on the fireplace mantle.

"Let's see what tomorrow brings. I'm on a new case that needs immediate attention."

"Come on, Chuck," she said as she leaned towards

him. "I say it's time for a break."

Chuck couldn't stop in the middle of a case and put things on the back burner. He was going to plow through this one.

Next morning, once Sharon left for work, Chuck was at the office where he asked Paula to bring him Jack's file. "I called Rayburn and he got us a name on the Ford Ranger plate," she said, smiling. "The name's Vernon Vetsky, nicknamed Mouse, and here's the address," she added, passing him a piece of paper.

"Criminal record?"

"Theft under."

"Good job. I'll check him out this afternoon. And when Matt gets in, ask him to try to find him. I'm heading out to Thorne's Law to work on Casey's embezzlement charges and..." Chuck scratched his chin, then grinned, "Leet's suspicious insurance claim. That paperwork ready?"

"Just like you asked. I even have the subpoenas ready for delivery tomorrow."

"You're a gem."

By the time Chuck walked out of Thorne's Law around 1 p.m., the sky had turned smoke-grey. He turned left on one of the city's three main arteries, Mountain Road, looking for the beige-coloured Ford Ranger. His mind wandered until his phone rang.

Matt's number. He flipped the phone open. "Hanley's Investigations."

"It's me, Chuck. Matt. I'm tailing that Ranger right now."

"Where?"

"Just past MacBeath on Mountain, heading east.

Where are you?"

"I'm stopping at the 7-Eleven on Mountain Road and Archibald. Stay on the phone with me."

A couple of minutes passed before Matt spoke again. "I'm behind him at a red light on Archibald and we're both behind a couple of cars. A soon as the light turns, I'll peel back and let you tail him."

Gazing straight ahead, eyes focused, Chuck saw the truck pass through the intersection and then saw Matt's car slow down, giving Chuck space and time to get behind the Ford.

Chuck followed the Ford's smudged red tail-lights, skidding around corners until he reached the Swamp Donkey pub.

A howling wind rose and a snow squall began lashing everything in sight. Chuck squinted and watched the parking lot through his busy wipers, saw a short, sallow skinny guy come out of the Ranger, his long forked beard and even longer hair slapping his face like baby eels. He waited for him to enter the pub before following. The sound of country music and the smell of fried food greeted Chuck at the door. He worked his way through the patrons and ordered a Coke.

Chuck scanned the pub and spotted his suspect huddled between two older men at the bar. The bigger one wore a leather vest and had tattooed biceps, and the other one, greasy hair, large ears and tattoos on the back of his neck. Chuck threw a toonie on the table when they stood to pay the waitress. He rushed to his vehicle.

Shortly after, the three men hurried out in fresh white snow. The Ranger driver, Mouse, was talking non-stop as the trio slowed next to the Ranger. Mouse jumped in, but the other two moved towards Chuck's vehicle. He put his head down, pretending to search for something, anything. As it turned out, he had parked between them. The bigger of the two drove a black pickup truck, license plate GIA 212 while the other one jumped into another black pickup, license plate CJX 416 and Storky's Waste Remediation Inc. written on the door.

❄

"I found Mouse and his friends," Chuck said as he sauntered back into his office. "They're bad-looking dudes. I'll get you those plate numbers."

"Sounds good, boss," Matt replied while digging through a file cabinet.

Cradling the phone on his shoulder, Chuck called Jack.

"When did you find him?"

"Just now."

"So who is it? And what else did you find out?"

"The guy driving the Ford Ranger is a skinny little rat with a drug problem. I saw him at the Swamp Donkey. He was hanging around two other guys – a big husky giant and a lean guy with long black hair, dark skin…"

Jack interrupted: "What about the guy I described to you? Was he there? He just looked like a normal guy, tall, but normal, with a beard. No dark skin. No tattoos, Chuck. Not a single tattoo on him. Where did they go after the pub?"

"Jack, they might not have anything to do with him. The truck just happened to drive up your street, who knows what they were doing there. I'll follow them some more and I'll get back to you." He paused for a breath. "I got their plate numbers. I'll get back to you in the next couple of days."

"Did you find anything on Scotsburn Road?" Jack asked.

"Not much," Chuck replied. "But I will."

Jack made an impatient noise. "Find out what the SOB drives, Jack. I want the bastard's name."

"Calm down now. I do have the license plate, but my contact at the detachment is out for a few days. I'll be in touch as soon as I find out."

"Don't call me!" Jack said before he hung up. "*I'll* call you."

CHAPTER EIGHT

A STUBBORN, UNABATED ARCTIC AIR MASS LINGERED over the region on Tuesday, February 18, the temperatures dipping to a 'real feel' of -38 Celsius with the windchill factor.

Ben stepped into the workshop and locked the door. He filled up the furnace and moved the rough-sawn bird's-eye maple boards closer to the electric, three-knife planer, threading each rough length steadily into the machine. He repeated the operation for all fifteen boards, shaving the wood down until they were all as smooth as stone. After stacking them, he took off his safety glasses and dust mask, and, although most of the wood particles had been removed by the dust collection system, he opened a window for a few minutes. The frigid air shocked his lungs.

Thank God for this job. The noise alone was enough to shut the world out.

Hunched over, his skilled hands ripped through the plywood sheets with precision until he had gathered enough pieces for the cabinet boxes. Ben then attached an 80-grit sandpaper disk to the hand-sander and turned it on, sweeping the hand-sander back and forth along the plywood. He then grabbed a tack cloth and wiped the plywood down. This would make it easier to take a coat of stain.

With drill in hand and pockets full of screws, he assembled the cabinets. When he finished, he walked into the house and sat, contentedly looking at the barely visible barbwire fence in the back yard. The sight made him think to the years when the acreage was farmland, in the early 1900s. He could envision hard times, but a simpler life, one with no bullies and where carrying a gun in plain sight was not only legal, but essential for one's safety.

After lunch, he grooved each cabinet door with a router, sanding rough edges and gluing the rails together tight and straight with clamps. They'd need time to take. He'd pick up from there tomorrow.

By mid-afternoon, he crossed the old, narrow, green-metal Gunningsville Bridge over the cold river into Moncton. He parked on Main Street and watched as pedestrian heads, bundled in earmuffs and toques, bounced up and down inside the tunnel-like sidewalks, each walled by five feet of snow.

He moved to Steadman Street, his eyes growing smaller and his gaze more intense as he stared at the brown brick building of the police headquarters. He imagined detectives sitting behind their cubicles or confronting suspects in interview rooms.

At 4:40 p.m., he walked into Don's Diner and took a seat in one of the red-vinyl booths by the window. Two older men at the neighbouring table talked about the upward spiral of gasoline prices and Bush's arrogance. A leathery-faced waitress approached, her dentures gleaming under the neon lights. She was probably too old to be wearing an undersized, white buttoned shirt and a black mini skirt, Ben thought, but who was he to pass judgement?

"Hi," she said in a scratchy voice. "Can I get you anything to drink?"

"I don't know yet," Ben said as he took one of the giant plastic menus from its rack.

Don's Diner had opened its doors in the late eighties and sat in the busy hustle and bustle of Mountain Road, a city street devoted mostly to fast foods and nightclubs. Pictures of Elvis filled almost every wall, alongside Marilyn Monroe, James Dean and the likes. A bubble gum machine stood proudly at the entrance next to the bar stools. And for a quarter, guests could rock n' roll down memory lane on the old Wurlitzer jukebox.

Outside, darkness fell but the diner blazed. A Moncton Transit bus, filled to capacity, interior lights illuminating its occupants, pulled next to a curb near the partially-enclosed glass bus shelter. The folding doors opened to the Arctic night, letting out a line of children, then mostly adults. Several people stood shivering outside, waiting to get on the bus as an old man came down the narrow anti-slip steps. Finally, he stuck his quad cane into the ground and took baby steps along the narrow path. Does he have a family? Ben thought. Is he going home to a cold house?

The waitress cleared her throat. "Ready to order?"

"I'll have the... fish cakes with... chocolate milk," he replied.

When the waitress left, Ben stared out the window and, although it was not in his nature to eavesdrop, he strained his ears and honed in on the two old gentlemen's conversation the next booth over.

"Now Wilbur, did you know that the community college is being used as a relief center?" one asked the other without waiting for a response. "They got room for five hundred people and it's full."

"Are you serious, Steve?"

Steve tapped the newspaper on the table. "Dead serious. And they're working round the clock to keep the pipes from freezing in schools."

"Not to change the subject," Wilbur replied, "but have you been to any of the public meetings about opening the causeway?"

"Nope," Steve continued, "but I'm all for opening the gates and bringing the river back to life."

"Not everyone shares your views, buddy," Wilbur said. "The Fishermen's Association in Alma thinks opening the gates is gonna mess up lobster fishing out in Shepody Bay."

"Personally," Steve said, "I think these studies are just a way for our government to stall it all so that they don't have to make a decision before the election in June!"

Ben devoured the meal knowing that his sister had cooked it. He sat in the restaurant until seven and waited for her shift to end. He turned his head when he heard the kitchen door open. His expression fell. Tina, a soda in one hand, approached with a limp, her eyes pink, lids sagging.

"My God, Tina. Are you okay?"

She sat across him with a trembling smile. "Yeah, I'm good," she replied in a hoarse whisper. "What brings you here? Did somebody die?" She pulled her baggy sweater tighter, hugging herself.

"I was hungry for your cookin', that's all," Ben replied with a smile.

Behind a head of limp and lifeless dull grey hair, Tina nibbled at a fingernail and then knitted her brows. She rubbed one of her bony shoulders and gave Ben a bleak stare. "Uh-huh. Are you on drugs or somethin'?"

"No. Why?"

She raised her chin for a moment and then put her head down. "Just the way you keep staring at the wall."

Ben twisted a teaspoon upright between his fingers. "How's Blackie?"

Tina glanced up from her lap, biting the inside of her cheeks. "He's fine... which reminds me, I'd better be getting home to feed him."

"Let me drive you," Ben said as he slapped a twenty-dollar bill on the table. "It's like walking in a deep freeze out there. Please, and this way I can see where you live."

She picked up her coat. "I'm used to the cold, and I've been stuck in this grease hole all day. Thanks, but I need the fresh air."

He watched as she stepped onto the sidewalk, her scarf wrapped tightly, stopping at a short distance away. She lit a cigarette and the smoke circled around her head. She turned and waved at him, her shadow tethered to her feet and stretched by the streetlights.

Visiting his sister was no different than the previous visits, still opening deep wounds that had never healed. Ben felt sorry for her and such thoughts made him feel guilty. He remembered a time when they used to take turns, Tony and him, pushing her around in a wheelbarrow filled with autumn leaves to make her laugh. His memories blurred and grew dark to another autumn day. Dad, his beard wild like the uncut grass around the house, had been home with Pete. They had borrowed a chainsaw to cut firewood and drank all morning. In the afternoon the duo headed for the woods. After a while, Mom ordered Tina to bring them some beer. Tina, peaches-and-cream complexion sprinkled with freckles, ran out the door with a bag of clinking bottles, her honey braids whipping in the air.

An hour passed before Ben went looking for her. He found her in tears by the edge of the woods, her dress torn. She couldn't walk so he half carried her inside and jumped the fence to a neighbours' house for help. Rod Cassidy had taken her to the hospital and nobody ever said a word about what happened that day.

As he pulled in his driveway at 9:00 p.m., Ben noticed fresh tire tracks and immediately stretched his right arm over the top of the passenger seat, turning his head to look through the rear window as he shifted to reverse. Bright lights blinded him. Ben shifted to park and stepped outside. Headlights shone in his eyes.

"Drive in!" a voice commanded.

"What do you want?" Ben shouted, fists on his hips.

He stared the car down until it backed out of the driveway and disappeared into the night. When he stepped inside the house, the stove's hood-light came on in the kitchen. He took in the scene: Mouse stood near the switch, smiling as if to say *gotcha*! At the same time, a lamp lit up in the living room, and then another in the hall.

"Have a seat, Bone Head," said Grinder deep in the Lazy Boy, feet propped up on the coffee table.

The door swung open behind him and a stranger entered.

Ben stood stiffly, arms crossed, and turned towards the stranger, a colossal monster bending his neck and shoulders to get through the doorway. "And who the hell are you?"

"Sit down," Grinder said with a cigarette hanging on his bottom lip. "We need to talk."

Ben rolled his eyes and sat on the edge of a couch in the living room. He tried to be calm and patient. Ben gave Grinder a cold look.

Grinder cracked his knuckles. "Meth'll be ready for you Friday night. At 10 p.m., a dark grey bin will be next to your mailbox for pick up. Be at the Lucky Strike bowling alley by 11 p.m., the one near Magnetic Hill, and go to the far end of the parking lot. There you'll see a woman in her twenties, a red head. She'll be waiting for you in a 1998 black Intrepid. Pull next to her and give her the pass code 'Galaxy.' When she replies with 'Ruby,' give her the bin and get the hell out of there. They're calling for heavy snow tomorrow, Bone Head, so there shouldn't be much traffic."

Ben didn't answer. He stared at the floor.

Mouse flicked the kitchen light switch on and off. "So where's the tape?"

Ben clenched his fists and held Grinder's gaze. "It's not here. I'll get it."

Grinder got up and squashed out his cigarette on a piece of firewood near the fireplace. "You certainly will," the wrinkles on his forehead growing thicker. "The girls already told us where your friend lives. Mouse, tell him what you did to the fur ball."

Ben snapped back, faking a laugh. "Mouse can't remember his own mother's name."

"Yeah, man," Mouse said. "I went there the other night to steal some stuff in the garage, but the thing was locked. So, I hid in the back of the house until the happy family came home. When they went inside the house, they left their freakin' yapping pooch out on the deck. I grabbed him and made a beeline for the garage. The fucker wouldn't stop barking, bit my freakin' hand when I covered his snout, so I slit his throat and threw him in the truck."

Ben stood. "Are you out of your mind?" He walked to the front door, opened it. "Get the hell out of my house!"

"How's your dog doin', eh?" Mouse said on the way out. The gang laughed.

The door shut and he stared through the window until the driveway went dark. Then, he lit a cigarette and stepped outside to a cold, inky black sky. He took a quick suck at the cigarette and tossed his head back and studied the Big Dipper and the North Star. He didn't feel the cold. He stretched his neck and leaned against the house, the smoke circling around his head, until his anger began to subside.

He returned to the workshop, and this time drilled holes for the pressed-in hinges and prepared the mouldings. He opened the window again before he began staining. He dipped the cotton cloth into oil stain and finished the doors first, wiping each one with an even coat, and then wiping with a dry cloth.

Wipe wet, wipe dry, wipe wet, wipe dry, and so it went for many doors and cabinet pieces. In a few days he'd apply the lacquer, and then call his boss at Cabinets to Go.

CHAPTER NINE

C HUCK WAS HEADING HOME WHEN HE STOPPED AT a traffic light. Outside the car, the cold wind was biting and a young couple, scarves wrapped tightly around their necks, stood at the busy intersection.

He remembered when this exact spot was a field where his aunt used to live. His mother would say they lived out in the boonies, but with exits to and from the highway nearby, it was now the retail heart of the city.

His stomach demanded supper and when the light turned green, he pushed hard on the accelerator. At that moment a half-ton truck, running a red light from the highway's off ramp, T-boned his passenger door, sending his vehicle against the lanes of traffic. The seat belt dug into his shoulder and the air bag punched his head against the top of the seat, but not for long. The vehicle tumbled before landing on its side in a small strip of field. Sheet metal bucked around him and everything went black.

When he came to, a powerful scent of burnt-chemicals hit his nostrils and he tried desperately not to smell it, tried to swing his head away, but he couldn't move. He had that unpleasant coppery taste in his mouth, too, the kind that makes you sick to your stomach. The wintry air gnawed at his face and began to freeze the liquid trickling over his forehead. His body ached.

Eyes shifting left to right, Chuck soon realized that he was pinned between the collapsing doors and the steering wheel. He drifted in and out of consciousness.

First came the sound of sirens and then fire extinguishers. After that, he recognized the sound of the Jaws of Life. He worried about igniting gas as he began smelling smoke, gasoline and radiator fluid. A buzzing noise filled his ears as the metal shears pushed their way through the passenger door. His heart beat faster.

He felt a sharp, stabbing chest pain that worsened on deep inhalation. Keeping his breath short, he closed his eyes as he was lifted and bundled. Then, there he was lying face up in an ambulance, hearing voices talk over him. He cast a blank stare at them. He couldn't make out what they were saying.

The next thing he remembered was waking up to the sounds of beeps next to his head and the sight of an IV dripping into his arm. He moved his fingers and toes.

"Mr. Hanley?" a female voice said. "Can you hear me?"

"Yes," he replied as her face became clearer. Chuck moaned. "Where am I?"

"You're in the ICU at the Moncton hospital."

"Why?"

"You had a serious car accident."

"Am I paralyzed?"

The nurse touched his shoulder. "The doctor will be in to see you shortly."

"What day is this?"

"Friday, February twenty-first."

Chuck tried to wiggle himself away from his restraints.

"A bit of patience, Mr. Hanley," the nurse said. "I'll get your wife if you want. She's sitting in a lounger next door."

"Please!"

Sharon pulled up a chair close to him, holding the bed rail with one hand and rubbing his arm with the back of her other hand. "Oh sweetheart."

"What happened?"

"You were in a car crash but you're doing really well."

"Feels like a dream."

She moved her hand up and rubbed his shoulder. "I know. You've had a collapsed lung and a concussion. And they've checked your spine for any damage. The doctor will be in soon to give us the results."

"How long have I been here?"

"Twenty-four hours."

"When can I go home?"

"Don't know, hon," she replied, smiling. "You'll have to wait for the doctor to tell us that. They've been very thorough so let's be patient for a while longer."

There were loud noises in the hallway as a nurse wrestled with a patient, trying to get him back to his room. Chuck stared at Sharon. And then a tall man, in his forties, with square shoulders and soft brown eyes, walked in wearing a white coat and stethoscope.

"Good morning," he smiled, "I'm Doctor Steiff, one of the ICU doctors here today. How are you feeling?"

Forcing a grin, Chuck said, "Great?"

"The good news is that you didn't break any bones or have any internal bleeding. You had a collapsed lung but we were able to re-expand it no problem. The only concern I have is your concussion. Concussions often cause dizziness and visual abnormalities for some time. If all goes well, we'll move you out of ICU to another floor and then home."

Chuck asked, "Was anyone else hurt in the crash?"

"Nothing serious. Any other questions?"

Chuck paused. "I feel like I'm in a fog...Am I on drugs? I'm so drowsy."

"Good question and, yes, we have you on pain killers – Percocet – for the time being, but we'll wean you off gradually as you start feeling better."

The lot in the industrial park was empty, and the large

warehouse stood quiet. Three men, in their early forties, sat in a cargo van nearby.

"You sure she told you exactly where those boxes are?" Mouse asked, lighting a cigarette and drawing deeply before blowing out a stream of smoke.

"Christ!" Rat replied, bending his head to stare him down. "You want out now? Get the hell out if you can't take the heat. I'm not in the mood!"

"You're always in a mood," Mouse replied, smoke shooting from his nose and mouth. "I'm in as soon as Grinder gives the okay, not you."

Grinder passed the headlamps to Rat and Mouse. "Knock it off... both of you. You're worse than kids. Put those on and follow my lead."

After strapping on snowshoes and three-hole ski masks, they trudged through the deep snow until they reached the back of the fabricated metal building. Mouse unfolded the ladder he was carrying on his back and laid it against the wall. Rat climbed the ladder with a hockey bag on each shoulder.

"Come on!" Grinder told Mouse. "Get up there and stick to what Rat tells you... and keep your walkie-talkies close."

Moments later, they reached the roof, the white cones of their headlamps beaming in the dark. Rat removed the oxy-fuel torch and heavy-duty drill out of his bag and cut through the steel roof. He rappelled down with a climbing harness and jogged fast to disable the alarm. Then, he flashed his light above for Mouse to follow. Once inside, they stood motionless for a moment, staring at the enormous pile of pallets in front of them.

"Take the far-right corner," Rat commanded as he pulled his mask up on his forehead and swivelled the headlamp, reflecting the light onto the boxes. "I'll start from the middle to the right and I'll meet you there. Use your sheet to find the numbers she gave us. Hurry!"

Mouse nodded, moving deeper into the warehouse.

Knives in hand, they sheared through boxes, shoving contents into their large backpacks. After fifteen minutes Rat ran over to his accomplice.

"Let's go," he commanded once again. "It's time."

Mouse continued to stuff smaller boxes into his bag. "I'm almost done!" A minute later they hooked their body harnesses to the dangling rope and pulled themselves back up.

Grinder was waiting for them. "Right on time," he said proudly, grabbing the stepladder. "Now run, ladies!"

The snowshoed trio laboured across the yard and, panting, reached the van. Grinder leaped into the driver's seat and arrowed out, driving back to the city. At a light, he fished his cellular out of his pocket and dialled.

"Part one is done! Dillies and Ox. Now heading to the big rig. Will meet others there."

Ten minutes later, they sat in their vehicle on the other end of town near a truck stop.

"Let me open it first," Grinder told the other two. "When I flash, send everybody down, you hear?"

Grinder slammed the van door and jumped the fence, making his way behind an eighteen-wheeler. There, he broke the plastic seal on the lock and dislodged the vertical bars in one quick crack. The trailer doors swung open.

He clicked the headlamp twice and a red blinking strobe flashed. Eight men joined him, their own beams cutting through the darkness. Rat opened the doors wider and kept guard while the men entered the truck box swaying as the men moved around in it, their breaths plumes of white steam. Grinder aimed the headlamp at the brown boxes inside and, with a box-cutter, sliced right through the strips of plastic tape. "Unpack each box and shove as much as you can in your hockey bags. Rat, get more empty bags in the van when you load these in."

An hour later, a convoy of vans snaked out of the truckers' stop and fled to the back roads of Albert County. A snow blower was clearing the parking lot as they arrived at the Trap House. They drove straight into the opened garage doors and unloaded the cargo. Five girls greeted them at the door.

Grinder shot them a startled look. "We'll be done in a couple of hours. Now, scram!"

Grinder then instructed his crew to open all of the boxes and start packing. Using clear plastic bags, they filled them with pills – Oxycodone, Methadone, Bezedrine, Ritalin, and Xanax. Once the goods were re-packaged, Grinder asked everyone to join him in the living room in the back of the camp.

"First line of business," he said, swinging a box of note cards in his right hand. "Spade, send these out tomorrow," he added as he threw the box at him.

"Yes boss," Spade replied.

"Look'a here," he said, hanging on to one of the girls by her waist. "Look at these beauties," he continued, sliding his large hand under her under shirt and pushing one of her large breasts completely out. He bent over and drove his head between her breasts, moaning. He then sat next to a large metal table and pulled her against him. Reaching under the table, he pulled out a bag of cocaine. "Fill your boots," he commanded as he tossed it to Rat.

Rat slit the bag open and poured cocaine on the coffee table. With a razor blade, he laid several tracks down. Each one took their turn snorting with a straw, while Grinder rubbed the cocaine on his gums. Within minutes, they were wide awake and fell into a deep, high-pitched trance as if going down an endless 90-degree hill on a roller coaster.

In the morning, the vans were returned to the rental agency and several of the misfits took their position at different locations in the city. Jay stood at his usual spot, an abandoned phone-booth near a high school, handing out pills, crack cocaine, and his pager number scribbled on pieces of paper. As soon as the lunch alarm rang, half a dozen kids rushed out to the booth, cramming their pockets with uppers and downers.

CHAPTER TEN

THERE WAS A LIGHT TAP AT THE DOOR AND BEN ignored it, hoping that whoever was there would go away. But they didn't; instead, the taps grew louder. Soon someone was banging on the door. He took a deep breath and swung the door open.

Spade got up in his face. "I'm here for the tape."

Ben's expression sobered; he didn't bother hiding his disappointment.

"Stay right there," Ben instructed, shutting the door on Spade. Within minutes, Ben returned, tape in hand. "Happy?"

Spade put a foot on the door step. "Not letting me in? It's freezing out here man."

"Better get a move on to your car then."

"Relax," Spade added in a soft voice. "I have a job for you."

Annoyed, Ben breathed deeply. "What job this time?"

Spade extended his arm, holding a large paper bag. "A delivery for Renous."

Ben shook his head in disgust. "You want me to go to the pen with dope? You take me for a fool?"

"No worries... we know the guards. It's all been arranged. Just show up the day after tomorrow and ask for Arnold Multimer. He works four to midnight."

"And how do I know you're not setting me up?"

Spade threw the bag at him. "Why don't you try not going and see what'll happen to you?"

Ben slammed the door hard, its extended thunder vibrating throughout the house. The dog stared at him. He was on autopilot, watching his life unfold for the benefit of others. He sat on the floor and plugged the earphones to the stereo, listening to "Against the Wind" by Bob Seger and the Silver Bullet Band.

After four hours of driving to deliver the goods at the Renous penitentiary, Ben returned home after dark, surprised that Bear wasn't at his usual spot at the door, nor did he hear his sharp barks greet him. He searched the house. His muscles tensed and his pulse quickened.

Ben walked over to the kitchen and kicked the dog's bowl. Then, he headed outside and lit a joint, numb against the cold. He knew the lost dog was no coincidence. He took a deep toke and closed his eyes, holding it before letting it go into the night. He drove to the Irving gas station in Hillsborough and parked behind the store, staring at the wide Petitcodiac River in the distance. After a while, he stepped out of the Jeep, shook a cigarette out of its pack and put one in his lips, lighting it. *Where would they keep Bear? Was he alive?* The dog would survive winter if left outside or even find his way back home, but where was he? He doubted they simply let him loose.

He dropped his cigarette and toed it out, then drove through back roads of Albert County until he reached the route leading to the Trap House. A halo ringed the cold night's moon. He parked a quarter of a mile from the target and set out on foot. After ten minutes, he smelled a whiff of wood smoke, and then he heard a bark. Yep, that was Bear. As he approached the Trap House, outdoor flood lights came on. He sneaked behind a large pine and stood still. Bear continued to bark and two guys came out, Spade and Mouse.

The dog growled.

Mouse unhooked him from the chain and clipped his collar on a leash, holding the one hundred and fifty-pound dog by the strap. Bear let out a high-pitched bark, and being bigger than Mouse by at least thirty pounds, twisted his body around until Mouse could no longer hold on to the leash. Bear ran straight to Ben.

"You fucker," Spade yelled. "Can't you do anything right?"

"Did you see the size of that thing?"

Chuck woke up, disoriented. His worst fear was to go blind. He opened his eyes and blinked until the room took shape. A television set perched on a dresser and further down he made out the door where sparkling necklaces dangled from a wooden peg. Then he heard the familiar sound of water running in the kitchen sink. He was lying on his back and turned on his side slowly.

He had a headache and felt bruised all over. How did he get home? He concentrated. Sharon had driven him home and she was no doubt doing the dishes. But she never did the dishes after dinner, only in the morning. Was it morning? His mouth was dry and he wanted something to drink. He heard the clatter of pots and pans and he slowly sat up on the bed, got to his feet and wobbled towards the door.

Once in the hallway, he spoke up. "Sweetheart?"

Sharon hurried to his side and wrapped her arm around his waist. "Good morning. How you feeling?"

"Awful. Glad to be home but just a wee bit stiff."

"You have a seat and I'll get some coffee going."

After breakfast, Chuck returned to bed, said he'd sleep through the last of his pain medication.

With the house quiet, Sharon snuggled up to a book but

getting past two chapters was a struggle. Worried thoughts coiled around in her head, thoughts like Chuck's job may be too dangerous and his accident may have been deliberate. Did someone want him dead? The loop continued. Would she lose him to a silly case? His only option would be to retire before it was too late.

Sharon tossed the book aside.

More coils. This time... about work... when she had closed Mrs. Helen Dempsey's eyes in Palliative Care the day before. Helen's children had brought all of their mother's medications from home, but Sharon, at the nurses' station, had to turn them away and let them know that their mother would have no use for those anymore. The blood had run out of their faces.

Helen had been a school teacher and, like so many before her, all too happy to tell her life story to a total stranger.

The frail woman had been stable when she'd arrived, but, as the days went on, she'd become confused, lost her appetite and finally took her last breath. It was comforting to know that, in some small way, she'd been able to help control Helen's pain through opioids, give her sips of fluids, and care for her as she crossed over. Helen had asked not to be subjected to cardiopulmonary resuscitation and, as predicted, she had accepted her departure long before her family did.

Sharon picked up a broom and swept the kitchen floor, busying herself with housework, never stopping until all of it was done – scrubbing the stains from her scrubs, doing laundry, dusting the furniture, washing the coffee pot, and cleaning the shower stall and bathtub.

At four o'clock, Sharon opened the pressure canner, washed four Cornish hens and set them in the pot in oil to brown. Her sister and brother-in-law would be in soon and Chuck would be beyond himself when he woke up to the smell of a freshly-cooked dinner.

She seasoned the birds with salt and pepper. In a separate bowl, she combined two cups of cooking wine, a Sauvignon Blanc, with chicken bouillon, thyme and parsley.

She secured the lid and placed the pressure regulator on the vent pipe, watching the pressure dial gauge climb to fifteen. Eight minutes and voilà, supper was ready.

Sharon heard the familiar squeak of the bedroom door. Within minutes Chuck walked into the kitchen.

"Why the long face?" he said to her.

"Oh… patients. You know me, I can't help it. I feel sorry for them. They get me every time."

He hugged her and dried the tear coming down her cheek.

"Switching departments may do you a world of good," he said as he walked away.

She caught up with him and poked him in the ribs. "I know I complain, but I like my job. And I worry about you. Wish you would retire."

He twisted her around and kissed her on the cheek before letting go of her. "Careful. You know I'm a sick man."

"Oh, don't I know it. How are you feeling?"

Chuck took a stool at the kitchen island, stretching. "I'm starting to feel back to myself. I just took the last of those pain killers so… I guess I'm good to go now."

CHAPTER ELEVEN

O N FRIDAY, MOTHER NATURE SURRENDERED ITS bitter wind-chill curse for a malediction of snow. At least 15 centimetres fell on doorsteps by noon.

Ryan Powers pulled his rig off the road by mid afternoon and parked it next to his coworkers' trucks in Atlantic Trucking Inc.'s yard, happy to spend some of his hard-earned cash at the Swamp Donkey. First, though, they'd have to meet the boss; it would be at least another hour before they could get their hands on a few beers and gawk at the topless girls delivering their meals.

The Swamp Donkey, a sleazy joint with weathered wooden shingles and shuttered windows, could at least boast its ironwork decor – traditional blacksmiths' tools, some anchored to the ceiling. Originally called The Foundry, the new owners had changed the pub's name but kept the décor. A drill press, at least a hundred years old, sat at the end of the bar, and next to it, metal shears, hammers, tongs and anvils. The best display of all, however, was newer, a life-size stuffed moose standing a short distance from the entrance.

The pub's floor was covered in peanut shells, and video lottery terminals glowed in a corner. A mass of smoke hovered over its sixteen tables, including the one with Grinder and his gang – Mouse, Spade, Rock, Q-Tip and Rat.

Ted Elkin, a mechanic, played darts with his pals Laurie King, Mike "Dodge" Wallace, Moe Green, and Bud, Ted's father-in-law. Steelworkers, machinists and welders from a steel fabrication outfit next door were also enjoying the break.

At 5 p.m., the truckers' meeting ended and several men walked out of the office, their feet slipping and sliding until they reached the sidewalk, ready to cross the road to the Swamp Donkey. Just as they were about to step onto the snow-covered pavement, a deafening blast dropped them to the ground. The earth shuddered and fragments of masonry and shreds of human flesh sailed upwards, soon followed by a rain of hot ash, glass, furniture, anvils and bodies. Lastly, a single weighty, biker-type boot landed near the sizzling communication lines by the road.

Ryan Powers, dazed, burn marks on his face, scrambled to his feet, his ears ringing, and called 9-1-1. Within minutes, cop cars, ambulances and fire trucks arrived, sirens blazing against the blacked-out street.

Sweat ran down Catherine d'Entremont-Simpson's face when her phone rang at 5:20 p.m. on Friday. She jumped off the treadmill and wiped her brow and neck with a hand cloth. Reaching into the open gym bag on the floor, she pulled out her Blackberry.

"Hello," she answered, out of breath.

"Cathy?"

"Diane?" she replied. "What's up?"

"You'll never believe this! An explosion just ripped through the Swamp Donkey on Airport Road. I'm standing in front of it now."

"What?"

"Yes!" she said. "You should see the mess. This is huge, Cat."

"On my way..." She paused before adding: "In the meantime, can you find Larry and get him to call me?"

In her early forties, Catherine was the superintendent of the Codiac Regional RCMP office in Greater Moncton. Her family life was not as successful as her career and may have had to do with the sixty hours a week she spent on the job. Her shoulder-length bright-toffee hair with wispy short bangs revealed her mother's pointy nose, full lips and soft complexion underneath, but her piercing blue eyes and high cheekbones came from the male side of the family – a generation of law enforcers going back as far as her grandfather, Alfred.

She rushed down to the changing room at the same pace she did everything else – in a hurry. On her way outside, she almost slipped on the pavement. *Snow, damn snow*, she murmured, *why did it have to snow*. Snow covered evidence and that's the last thing anybody wanted right now.

Diane, a tall, promising new recruit, quickly approached Cathy when she arrived at the scene.

"Diane," Cathy said, shaking Diane's hand. "Did you call Larry?"

"He's working out of the Halifax office these days. He'll be on the first flight to Moncton in the morning."

"Thank you. So what do we know so far?"

Diane, pointing at a building across the Swamp Donkey, said, "A few men, who work across the street at JMA Trucking, were on their way to the pub when the bomb – if it was a bomb – went off. They're still at JMA if you want to talk to them."

Cathy shook her head. "No... no need to. All they saw is the explosion, right?"

"That's right."

"Set up the perimeter... please," Cathy said, trying to make sense of the scene. "And also get tarps and cover as much evidence as you can. Damn snow is our biggest enemy."

She stood by the street, staring in awe at what used to be the Swamp Donkey. It now had holes in the walls and windows, the back wall blown out and distorted.

CHAPTER TWELVE

As soon as Sharon left for work that night, Chuck steered the rental vehicle through city streets, finding his way to Jack's home. Snow fell steadily like freshly harvested sheep's wool, giving the small street the appearance of a soft, fleecy, Sherpa blanket in no time. He pulled in the empty driveway. The garage's motion-activated lights came on and in his rearview mirror he noticed Randy's house across the street. It was still lit up like a Christmas tree. He stepped through the calf-high snow to the front door.

Just as he rang the doorbell, he saw a gap in the door. He gave the door a slight push. It moved a few inches. He then pushed it with his shoulder, but it didn't budge any farther. He widened his feet, and, holding on to the casing, leaned forward and groped his right hand inside the house. After a bit of searching, his index finger found a switch. He wormed his way through the opening.

"Holy smokes," he murmured, covering his nose as he jerked his gaze away from the floor for a moment. The odour was striking and his pulse quickened. He pulled a handkerchief from his coat pocket and put it over his nose and his mouth. His teeth clenched as he saw Jack's body on the floor; he was on his back and still in winter apparel. One of his feet rested stiff against the door. Jack's face was livid, his jaw gaped and a clean slash of a blade had made its way around his neck. Chuck slipped out for much-needed air and reached for the phone in his coat pocket. After dialling 9-1-1, he parked his vehicle on the street. What was going on here? Did Jack share everything? *Another slit throat...the dog, then Jack.* The siren startled him. Chuck stepped out of his rental to meet the cop.

"Are you the one that called 9-1-1?"

"Yes," Chuck replied, offering a brief handshake. "I'm a former cop... Chuck Hanley's the name." Chuck thought the cop looked young, a rookie most likely.

"What did you find?"

"A dead body at the front door and I didn't go any further. Didn't want to tamper with evidence. Here's my card."

"Until I check the place, I need you to take a seat in the cruiser. Please."

"No problem," Chuck replied on his way to the officer's car.

The cop pulled his gun out and rushed to the front door, slipping through the opening like a string though a needle. The house lit up, and, moments later, he ran outside and vomited near the front door before returning to the cruiser.

As soon as the young cop sat in front of Chuck in the cruiser, Chuck said, "Your first time?"

"Do you know this family?" he asked Chuck as he rubbed a hand against the front of his coat over his heart. He was white as a ghost.

"Only the guy on the floor. He was my client," Chuck replied from the back seat. Chuck searched the cop's face, thought he saw a flicker of distress. "Who else was in there?"

"You hang in there for a while longer, Mr. Hanley." The young cop stepped out of the car and put the phone to his ear.

Chuck did the same, dialled home and left a voicemail to his wife. "It may be a long night. Don't worry if I'm not home in the morning. I'll probably be at the cop station. Call you as soon as I can. Love you."

"Seems that you check out," the cop said as he got back into the cruiser. "I found three more bodies inside – two women, and a baby."

"Sweet Jesus," Chuck swore under his breath.

In no time, a small crew of white suits descended on the residence. Chuck's phone rang.

"Where are you?" Sharon asked. "I leave you home and you disappear. Are you okay?"

"I'm fine," Chuck replied.

"Why aren't you answering the home phone? Tell me you're not out."

"Sorry, sweetie. Police work. You know me; it couldn't wait and I'm fine. Stop worrying so much."

"Chuck Hanley," she pleaded with him. "Go home and stay home. You know you shouldn't be out. Rest is what you need."

"Yeah, I know," he replied. "Got something I want to look into and I should be home by the time you get back in the morning."

"Careful," she added. "*Please*, be careful."

Randy opened the front door to check the disturbance across the street and recognized the man walking towards his house. The hurling wind kicked the snow all around as Randy stepped out on the porch.

"Chuck!" Randy said, squinting. "What brings you out here?"

"Tragedy across the street," Chuck replied, his feet making fresh tracks in the snow. "It looks like a quadruple homicide." Chuck kept his head down, away from the wind biting at his cheeks.

"What?" After a moment, Randy swore, then invited Chuck in, taking his arm and guiding him to the open front door.

"Sorry to come over unannounced," Chuck said.

"Nonsense," Randy said as he took Chuck's coat. Randy's wife Sheila approached, hand over her mouth.

"Long time no see, Sheila. Though I'd rather it be under different circumstances," Chuck said.

They went to the living room window, arms crossed as they watched ambulances fill up with body bags.

"Mind giving us a few minutes, Sheila?" Chuck asked while scrutinizing the exterior.

"Not at all. Can I get you anything?"

"No thank you."

"How well do you know your neighbours?" Chuck asked Randy.

"I know them well enough. We both coach minor hockey. He works for the power company, his wife just had a baby... and the mother-in-law moved in a year ago, I think."

Chuck made a face and swallowed before continuing. "They're gone. All of them from what I've heard."

"That's... *Who'd would want to kill people like that?*" he asked not expecting a reply, his face lost in tears. "Sheila was becoming good friends with the mother-in-law. Florence."

"Do they have any family around here?"

Randy watched the last ambulance's doors shut, then watched the vehicles, lights not flashing, slowly pull away. "His parents," Randy replied. "He's from the east coast. Parents just left for Louisiana, I think. He went to wish them bon voyage last weekend."

"What about her?" Chuck asked.

"Her father's dead and, like I said, the mother moved in with them permanently. A sweet little old lady."

Chuck recommended the couple lock their doors, just to be safe, then headed for the RCMP station on MacBeath Avenue.

"I'm looking for Cathy d'Entremont-Simpson," Chuck said to two cops behind the bulletproof walk-up window.

"Your name, sir?" one of the constables said through the voice port.

"Hanley?" the other veteran said as he stepped out in the lobby. "Remember me? Hipson?"

"Nope," Chuck replied, scratching his head.

"Robert... Rob," he added. "I'd only been here a month before they shipped me to Newfoundland. But I was here when you arrested Jack Cornwall for trafficking."

"And you're idling behind a glass now?" Chuck inquired, smiling.

"Pulled a guy over, drunk driver barrelled into us," he replied. "Lucky it was only one leg..." he paused lifting the bottom of his trousers showing an artificial leg.

Chuck nodded slowly. "Sorry to hear that."

"You retired now?" Rob asked.

"No, just opened my own business as a PI."

"Nice. Wait here. Let me call upstairs for Catherine."

CHAPTER THIRTEEN

BEN WOKE UP YAWNING AND RUBBING HIS CRUSTY eyelashes Friday morning. The house was cold, but at least Bear was back. He smiled as he stroked Bear along the spine as he lay next to him in bed. "Yeah, you're a good boy."

Ben then built a fire bed with kindling and newspaper, touched the lit, wooden match to a corner of the paper. While the blaze picked up, he turned the coffee pot on and walked outside and down the driveway to the mailbox. He shoved the plastic-covered newspaper under his arm and smoked a cigarette on his way back. Light flurries danced around his head.

Coffee in hand, he fed the fire and settled down at the kitchen table to read the daily, but he couldn't focus. He turned the pot off and filled the stove to the brim, this time stepping outside with Bear. He walked the dog to his neighbours' place and asked if they could keep him for a couple of days, long enough for him to find Bear a safe place.

He wrestled with broken branches frozen to the ground on the driveway, then walked inside, threw a few logs over the pile and by nine o'clock snowmobiled up to the aircraft.

He flew above swathes of backcountry, the landscape shining like white quartz. He spotted a few horseback riders meandering on snow-white trails in the woods. Flying over Fundy Park, he spotted Dickson Falls just a half kilometre off Point Wolfe Road, and the broad curtain falls, Laverty

Falls, where he'd swum as a teenager. He swore he could hear their roaring power.

Feeling liberated, he stretched his neck, letting the kinks vacate his body. His shoulders dropped and his mind reeled back to his younger days when they'd bike to Fundy in summer. The ride was long, hilly, sometimes even dangerous with all the tourists and their idiotic campers on the road, but he had fun.

He began his descent to a frozen mud road in early afternoon and barely landed the plane, given the short distance. The snow was getting a bit thicker. He stepped out of the aircraft and was greeted by stiff, cold air. He inhaled deeply, feeling alive as the adrenaline rush began to subside. He stood in silence against a backdrop of snow-packed trees. An eagle soared above and he listened to the stillness, slowly shutting off those pesky thoughts.

From his fleeting state of bliss, he could see the big picture, and ending it all against a mountain started to make sense. Grinder would lose his grip on him. But, no, that meant folding, giving up on his family... and he wasn't ready to do that.

With his stress lightened a bit, he hit the dull grey late-afternoon sky again and, after a couple more hours airborne, he returned to earth, where his snowmobile's tracks soon turned up a new layer of fresh snow and led to his ribbon-shaped driveway.

Home, he tilted his head skyward and caught a few fluffy flakes on his tongue, his face open and happy. He tended to the fire and with a full stomach plowed the driveway and sat back in front of the tube. He hated the thought of going to town for a damn delivery. Television on mute, he flipped through the channels, trying to kill time.

He inhaled a puff of hashish and coughed it out as quickly as it went in when he saw a picture of a partially snow-covered Swamp Donkey sign beside the smoking wreckage. He turned the volume up, but the broadcast on the event was over. He channel-hopped, but nothing. He bounced to the kitchen and turned on the radio. Nothing. He then called Tina. No answer. She won't be home for at least another half hour, he thought. He paced the floor, scratching his head.

He tried Tina's number again and, this time, left a message on her voice mail.

"It's me," he said. "I realize you're not home yet, but please call me as soon as you get this."

Once he hung up, he called next door. His tenant, Ken, picked up quickly.

"Ben! How's it going? Enough snow for you?"

"Listen!" Ben blurted out. "What the heck happened to the Swamp Donkey?"

"It's all over the news."

"What happened?"

"I guess somebody blew up the Swamp Donkey."

"Anybody hurt?"

"Are you kidding me? Pretty sure nobody made it out alive."

The Swamp Donkey was Grinder's pub. *Could Grinder have been there when it happened?*

Ben jumped into the shower and slipped his jeans on and a white T-shirt. He walked outside at 10:00 p.m. and was caught off guard by the heavy snowfall and the wind. He turned back and threw on a western-type canvas jacket. He broke a path to his car through the snow drifts and brushed the snow off the windshield, the windows and the hood. He drove to the end of the driveway and picked up the bin underneath his mail box, returning to the house long enough to transfer the drugs into a guitar case and turning the bin upside down on the deck.

He then left, driving on the quiet Route 114. On his way to town, the radio blaring, a roadblock appeared out of nowhere. He pulled behind several cars, waiting to get through, the windshield wipers sweeping in a steady motion. When his turn came, the officer checked his license and registration and then let him go. As he drove to Moncton, his thoughts flickered between Maryel and the pub.

He arrived in town frazzled – a man looking for answers. Most nights, Main Street was empty, but tonight it was bumper to bumper traffic moving at the pace of a canoe. He drove by the RCMP detachment on Main Street where at least twenty cruisers lined the adjacent cul-de-sac, not to mention the press crowding the front door.

He pulled the Jeep to the curb across the street. Biting the inside of his lips, he stared out the window at the moving headlights.

If Grinder and his miserable gang had been in the pub, his life would return to normal. Maryel would move back in. He let out a sigh of relief... then held his breath. But whoever blew up the pub could come after him, too. After all, he was part of the gang, wasn't he? Should he talk to the police? Would they believe his story? Would his plea for protection backfire? "I'm no angel, either," he murmured. The more he thought about it, the more he felt the urge to stay away.

He checked the car clock. 10:30 p.m. If he didn't hurry he'd be late for the delivery.

He swung by Airport Road and slowed as he drove by what was left of the Swamp Donkey, now cordoned off with flapping yellow tape. He turned around and headed for the other end of town in search of a black car at the bowling alley, but there were no cars in sight as he entered the parking lot. The big neon bowling pin sign in the front of the building stood unlit. Outside, the sticky snow kept falling, drifting around his vehicle, filling his windshield. He waited until 11:30 p.m. and left.

For a short distance, he followed a city truck squirting salt on the road ahead, and his gas light came on. He stopped at an Ultramar and lifted his collar up as he pumped gas. While at the cash, a news clip of the Swamp Donkey scene appeared on the television set high on a corner shelf of the store.

"Sir!" a teenaged clerk, with rings in his nose and

eyebrows, said, trying to get Ben's attention. "That'll be thirty dollars."

Ben handed him forty and continued to stare at the TV.

"I don't know what the hell is going on this city," the teen noted as he turned his head towards the television. "The pub got all blown up and a family on my street got killed. All hell broke loose in this town last night, man!"

"A family?" Ben said, surprised.

"Yeah, we were totally stunned by it," he added. "Just got off the phone with my Dad. Said the cops just interviewed them to see if they saw anything unusual."

Ben's blood ran cold. "What street do you live on?"

"Hazelton Estates," the cashier replied, giving Ben a strange, 'what rock have you been under' look. "The guy worked for NB Power. They just had a baby and last weekend he came around looking for his dog. My dad said the whole family was carried out of the house on stretchers."

"What's this guy's name?" Ben asked. "Do you know his name?"

"Thibodeau" the cashier replied. "Jack Thibodeau. The whole story is in the paper," he said while pointing at the newspaper stand.

Ben shook his head, lost for words. His mind replayed Jack, the whole mess of it. Knocking him out, the videotape. How had he gotten so far into this? He took the paper and waited for the cashier to return his change. He wanted to run.

He couldn't go home now. They could be waiting to do him in, too. He drove around town, swerving around finger drifts on the deserted streets. He wanted to go to the cops, but not with drugs in his vehicle. He needed time to think. He gunned down to a motel on the outskirts of town, signing in as Gerry Brown. He paced the floor of his room. After a while, he opened the curtains and stared at his snow-blanketed Jeep. He finally settled down long enough to read the paper and fell asleep in the early hours of the morning.

At dawn, he spread the newspaper across the bed and re-read every single word about the crimes. The whole family. Who was he up against?

The snow had just stopped when he jumped in a waiting taxi. With a steady and confident pace, he walked up to the police station.

CHAPTER FOURTEEN

SATURDAY MORNING. 6:30 A.M. PATHOLOGIST DR. Gail Patrick sets foot into the morgue after only a few hours of sleep. The dim room is full of bodies and body parts – gashed, torn to shreds, charred. Each piece was tagged during the night by her forensic team and identified by weight, length, hair and eye colour, condition of clothing, possessions and any special markings – scars, tattoos. Each piece will be photographed and x-rayed until it becomes an online patient file. A file, not even in hard copy, is what's left of a life.

She flips the switches that light the ceiling a row at a time.

The next rotation will arrive in less than two hours. And, while most people would find the sight creepy, she, on the other hand, has become immune to it. At her age, her nose has adjusted and the gag reflex is all but gone. She knows she can get at least three of the less beaten ones done by lunch time. Chest, abdomen, brain. Chest, abdomen, brain, she repeats to herself. She turns on every light in the room and dives in. First, she cuts a Y-shaped incision into a body, running across each shoulder down to the pubic bone and then separating the skin and underlying tissues to expose the rib cage and abdominal cavity. His throat has been slashed, no doubt the cause of death, but she ignores that for the moment and continues her examination. Scalpel in hand, she removes the front of the rib cage and all that lies underneath – the windpipe, the thyroid and parathyroid glands, esophagus, heart, and lungs. Then, she moves down, taking out the abdominal organs. Next, she cuts through the back of the skull from one ear to the other. Using a vibrating saw, she removes the top of the skull, where she gently lifts out the entire brain. She puts aside all organ samples to be examined under microscope by her staff.

It's 7:30 a.m. now and five eager pathologists, flown in from all parts of Atlantic Canada, walk in to the smell of death.

"Welcome!" Karen says with a tight-lipped smile. "Thank you, each and every one of you, for agreeing to let me take you away from your busy schedules. We don't have much time, so let's get right down to it. We have an unusually large number of corpses, and, sadly, a lot more body parts. Follow me."

She pauses and then they trail behind her to the coolers. She gives a briefing and opens the floor for discussion. A flurry of questions ensues, and, at some point, she stops and turns on her heels.

"Well, then, shall we get started? Holler if you need help."

From the stainless-steel cooler, one of the technicians pulls out the tiny cadaver wrapped in a white sheet, and places it on a cold iron slab, the tiny head too small for the adult headrest. The circulating assistant compares the tag number with the paper on her clipboard. She gives the okay. A beautiful angel in a red-purplish casing. The small coffin would be the heaviest to carry.

Just as early that morning, Larry White, a veteran detective from Halifax, arrived at the Codiac detachment while an RMCP helicopter hovered over the city, waiting to respond to any emergency. Teams of cops, with their track dogs, were posted at roadblocks, pulling over random vehicles for questioning. Only three of the city's main arteries were cleared and snowplow crews, working overtime, pushed hard to open the rest of the city. The events sparked rumours that spread through the masses. Newspaper sales soared, and, under the watchful eye of a thirsty public, a media firestorm ignited.

Cathy walked into her office early morning and stepped up to a large window overseeing the city. She closed her eyes for a moment and wondered where the city would put all that snow. Quickly, a wave of anxiety hit her. Would she find the murderer or murderers? Who else was at risk? Her list of worries had only begun, but when Larry walked in her anguish faded.

"Hi," Cathy said, beaming as she extended her arm for a hand shake. "It's so nice to see you again and thank you so much for agreeing to help us out."

"Sounds like you'll need all the help you can get."

"Indeed. Please have a seat."

"How you holding up?"

"As well as expected. Can I get you anything? Coffee, water...?"

"No, I'm fine, thanks."

"Then let me cut right to the chase and start by showing you a few pictures and fill you in on the situation. And let me add that Chuck Hanley, one of ours, but now a PI, was hired by Jack Thibodeau, one of our Hazelton Estates' victims, to find a guy that, Thibodeau said, held him captive for a few days in Albert County."

"Okay..."

They went over the facts, and half an hour had passed when Catherine's phone rang. It was Diane. "I have Deputy Commissioner Alan Terry on the line. Can I put him through?"

Cathy nodded to Larry. "Let me get this and just listen in," Cathy said as she cradled the phone under her chin.

She listened to Alan's invitation to a meeting that afternoon and watched Larry as he flipped through pictures of the recent crimes.

"I'll be there," Cathy said to Alan before she hung up. But just as they were about to restart the conversation, the phone rang again.

"A guy by the name of Ben Walsh is in the lobby," the officer stated on the phone. "Says he's got information on Jack Thibodeau."

"Okay. Bring him to the audio/video interview room next to my office. Thank you."

Cathy looked up at Larry. "This should be interesting. Someone's here to talk about Jack. Hang on for a minute," she added as she picked up the phone and dialled Diane, asking her to call Chuck and get him here.

"So this is the Thibodeau you've been talking about?" Larry asked.

"Yes," Cathy said, her eyes widening.

Larry leaned in. "Can I interrogate Ben?"

"Sure, but let's wait for Chuck... he's been involved for a while."

"Fine by me."

A few minutes later, grim-faced Ben, with his coat under his arm, walked into the interview room adjacent to Cathy's office. Behind the one-way mirror, Cathy and Larry studied him until Chuck arrived.

"Good morning," Chuck said as he walked into Cathy's office.

"Chuck, meet Larry. Larry, meet Chuck."

While the men shook hands, Cathy asked them to join her near the one-way mirror. "Does this guy look familiar, Chuck?"

"No," Chuck replied. "I've never seen him before."

"Ben Walsh," Cathy said. "He just came in to talk to us about Jack Thibodeau."

"Are you serious?" Chuck said. "Can't wait to see what he has to say."

Chuck and Cathy watched as Larry walked into the interview room and introduced himself to Ben.

"And you are?"

"Ben Walsh."

"Can I see some I.D.?"

Ben handed Larry his wallet. "Here's my driver's license. Is that enough?"

Larry studied the license for a few seconds without speaking, looked at Ben and then returned the wallet. Pointing a finger at the ceiling, Larry said, "We have video and audio recording in here. Are you okay with that?"

"Sure," Ben replied. "I can't see why not."

"Okay then, let's get started. For the record, I'm Detective Larry White and today is Saturday, February twenty-third at 8 a.m. I'm here with Benjamin Walsh, born February fourteen, 1958."

"Call me Ben, please."

"Alright, Ben. So what information do you have on Jack Thibodeau?"

"I'd like to start from the beginning if you don't mind."

"Go ahead."

Over the next five minutes, Ben spilled the beans on his predators to Larry – the pig roast where it all began the previous summer, the drugs and the prostitutes. Ben's face burned with embarrassment when he talked about the video he'd shot of Jack while he had him under the influence of Rohypnol.

Larry straightened his back and stopped the interview. "Do you realize that you may be putting yourself in jeopardy by going any further with your story?"

"Yes, I realize that, but the idea of having someone kill me sounds much worse."

"Can you confirm that you are giving your statement freely and voluntarily?"

"Yes," Ben replied. "I am."

"Do you also realize that your statement may be used as evidence against you in a court of law?"

Ben tugged at his chin. "Yes, but I have nothing to hide. That's why I'm here."

"Okay," Larry said. "Go on."

"About Jack, I did it to cover my ass. You don't know them like I do."

"Who are we talking about, Ben?"

"I'll get to that." Next, Ben told the story about a night in 1971 disclosing what he called "an old family secret" – the burial site of his father's remains in the horse barn beside his house.

"This is the guy who held Jack Thibodeau hostage?" Chuck asked. "Strange for him to waltz in here like this."

"Where are you from, Ben?" Larry asked calmly.

"Weldon," he swallowed as he picked a paper clip off the floor and opened it, trying to take the kinks out of it. "133 Scotsburn Road, off the 114. I haven't been home since Friday night. I stayed at the Red Dragon Motel and took a cab straight here this morning. Like I told you, I'm scared they'll come after me next."

"Do you work?"

Ben kneaded his fingers. "I'm a cabinet maker."

"You live alone."

"Yes."

"If I patted you down, would I find anything? Any drugs?"

"Yes," he replied. "Well, no, not on me, not here," he added as he tapped his fingers on the table."

"Okay, now, do '*they*' have names?" Larry asked, raising his eyebrows.

"They're a low life, redneck gang and I don't know the head honcho's real name," he replied. "I've always ever known him as Grinder, but I went to school with Mouse. His name is Vernon Vetsky. And then there's Rock Durel, goes by the name of Rat. Then Spade. Don't know his real name either, but I think he's native. And Robert Shaw, the junkie. Everybody calls him Q-Tip because he lost a bet at some point and now he dyes his hair white. They've been at it for a very long time. They're the ones who put the pig roast on every year. They hang out at the Swamp Donkey pub when they're not at their camp they call "The Trap."

"Tell me more about the drugs," Larry continued. "Where are they?"

Ben sat up in his chair and looked Larry straight in the eye. "They drop off a package at my house on a regular basis and tell me where to take it. I store the drugs in guitar cases until it's time for delivery."

"Okay," Larry said. "Let's take a break. I'll be right back."

"Ring any bells, Chuck?" Cathy asked.

"None other than Jack had given me the address where he thought he was held. 133 Scotsburn Road. Found a Jeep in the driveway and ran his plates. That *is* him."

"He's scared," Larry stated. "That I know for sure."

"What else do we know about this guy?" Cathy inquired. "Why haven't we seen or heard from him before?"

"Chuck," Cathy said. "Please go in with Larry and show him your photos, from the pub before the explosion. Let's see if he recognizes any of them."

Chuck grabbed his laptop and within seconds Cathy was watching him introduce himself to Ben. He set the laptop on the table. "Do any of these guys look familiar to you?" Chuck asked as he clicked on the mouse and turned the laptop towards Ben.

One by one Ben identified Grinder, Mouse, Spade, Rat, Q-Tip and Long Beard.

"And this guy?" Larry asked as he displayed Jack Thibodeau's photo on the screen.

Ben sucked in a breath. "That's Jack Thibodeau. Look, I didn't kill any of them..." Ben trailed off and then seemed to remember he was talking. "Do you think I'd be crazy enough to do that and come here this morning?"

"Did you wear a goalie mask when you had Jack at your house on Valentine's Day?" Chuck asked.

"Well...yes... but..." Ben replied. "Can I explain?"

"By all means," Larry replied.

"I didn't want him to see my face," Ben continued. "I'm the victim here. They're the bad guys, not me."

"Do you own any weapons?" Larry asked.

"Yeah," Ben said. "A .48 that my father brought home one day when I was a kid. He killed our dog with it target shooting in the back yard. He was a drunk. I found it a few years ago in the attic when I renovated my mother's house. It's hidden in the heat register in my room."

Larry got up and Chuck followed. "That's it for now, Ben."

"Does that mean you're going to help me?" Ben asked quietly.

"It all depends. You're certainly not under arrest for anything – we corroborate this information – but I can't make any promises."

Not long after, Larry returned.

"Listen, we're going to check your hotel room, your vehicle and your house. Meanwhile, given what may be waiting for you outside these doors, I suggest it best that you sit still until your information checks out. Okay?"

Ben replied with a sigh of relief. "Hopefully, they can't get to me in here."

Ben freed his keys from his pants' pocket. "Be my guest. Can you do me a favour and turn up the thermostats when you're there...to keep the pipes from freezing?"

"We can do that," Larry said, nodding. "Sign here; it'll give us authority to search your house." Larry handed him a piece of paper.

Cathy dropped her keys on the hall table as she entered the condo. She glanced at her silhouette in the mirror and brushed her hair away from her face. She frowned at the crow's feet radiating from the corners of her eyes and mouth. She walked over to a large bookcase in the living room and sifted through photo albums, pulling one out and sitting back on the edge of the sofa to examine it.

Her index finger tapped on a picture showing Pierre,

her ex, with Larry and his wife Annette. Larry and Annette were holding each other around the waist, and Pierre had his arm around her shoulder. She sighed. She wished things had been different with Pierre, but she was so young when they met, and people change. At least she had. She'd needed more to life than cooking or having children. Being in his shadow.... She and Larry had worked together on a case in the early eighties, and this picture was taken at a banquet where both were decorated with honours. Larry's powerful physique, at six feet three inches, prevailed. She returned the album to the bookshelf before making her way to the bathroom.

She undressed and threw her clothes in the hamper. Then, she turned the taps on in the bathtub, pouring field-berries sea salt under the water fall. The softness of the floor mat felt soothing under her feet. She slid open one of the rattan basket drawers in the tallboy next to the mirror and pulled out two towels; one for her hair and one for her body, hanging them on the towel rack next to the tub. She submerged into the bath water, letting her right foot dance under the spout until the bath was full.

Larry's wife had died in a car accident two years ago. His last words today had been, "Don't hesitate to call if you need me."

She had butterflies just thinking about him for God's sake. "Slow down, Catherine," she murmured to herself as she closed her blue eyes and absorbed the warmth of her surroundings.

CHAPTER FIFTEEN

B Y 10:00 A.M. SATURDAY, BEN'S HOUSE SWARMED
with a crew of law enforcement personnel and
forensic experts. Diane headed upstairs to the master
bedroom. She scanned the room – it was neat, nothing out of
place. The bed was made and the curtains drawn. One hard-
shell guitar case leaned against the far wall of the bedroom.
She crossed the room and peered through the bedroom
window where she spotted a side entrance down below.

"Don't forget to dust the guitar case," Diane said,
pointing to it as she passed by one of the cops in the hallway
and headed behind the house. "Inside and out."

Once prints were recovered from the upstairs, the
forensic team moved to the basement, scanning for bits of
hair, blood and fingerprints on cupboards, furniture, toilets
and showers.

"I'm disappointed," Diane said to Larry as they
regrouped in the kitchen. "We have the gun but no mask."

Larry nodded, then asked, "What did you find
outdoors?"

"Nothing," she replied. "Just firewood. You?"

"Found a receipt book," Larry said, "and monthly
cheques to Ben for $400 from a Ken Lewis." When Diane
furrowed her brow, Larry added, "He must have a rental
property. Can you get me Ken's number?"

"I'm on it."

Outside, Don Foster and his assistant, Denis Whalen,
examined the horse barn. Whalen, a rookie forensic

anthropologist, measured the building and wrote down the material he would need for his search. He seemed excited, saying that it was going to be "a piece of cake."

"You're lucky, Denis," Don responded. "It's rare for people to walk in off the street and tell the PO-lice where to find a body. But don't get *too* excited, it's going to take us a while just to prepare the site to start digging. Dr. John Taylor from St. Thomas' anthropology department is joining us and will be in charge of the exhumation and, from what I hear, Dr. Gail Patrick will be tagging along."

"I know her," Denis noted, smiling. "She's a funny character."

"That's Gail," Don commented. "Then you also know to stay out of her way. Both are very competent. So just sit back and learn."

The prep work and the search for Gerald Walsh's body continued throughout the evening with a few more crime-scene technicians arriving at Ben's house with their equipment. They helped Denis set up a forensic tent outside the front door to the barn and lent a hand emptying the barn of its firewood, to the protests of a squirrel who had taken up residency. In the meantime, Don sprayed Luminol in near-total darkness, and quickly the inside walls and floor planks glowed blue. While Don took samples off the planks, Denis videotaped the area under surveillance.

Powered by a gas generator, bright flood lamps hung from the ceiling and heaters warmed up the place. Denis kept clicking the camera. With careful attention to detail, Diane removed the twelve grey, mouldy floor planks, and one by one laid them on a sterilized tarp. She then attached a numbered plastic tie to each plank in the same sequence they had once lain in the barn. By midnight, they all left for coffee and donuts in Hillsborough while a cop stayed behind to keep an eye out for looters.

When they returned, Gail, a petite woman dressed in a deep-purple, one-piece snowmobile suit, stood outside the barn waiting for them. She wore a stocking hat with the tail wrapped around her neck. Next to her was Dr. Taylor, a stocky man with bright copper hair and curling eyebrows. Neither one said much, but both worked hard. By 6 a.m. on Sunday, the digging paid off and revealed the remains of a body in less than fourteen inches of dirt. Each bone was examined closely before being put in clear, sterilized bags. Once all of bones were compiled, and the body assembled in the back of Dr. Taylor's SUV, he drove off to perform a post-mortem in Moncton.

Diane took a deep breath and leaned against her car door. A few feet away, Gail started her car and Diane walked over. "How old is the corpse... do you know?" Diane asked.

"No idea yet. It takes between eight to twelve years for a body to decompose when it's been buried without a coffin or embalmed. We'll do more testing, then we'll have a much better idea."

"Male or female?" Diane probed.

"The jawbone is large and pronounced which is typical of a male, but again, we can't give you a definite answer yet. Dr. Taylor is the real expert here and it's in his hands now."

"Forgive my impatience, and thank you," Diane said. When Gail drove off, Diane settled behind the wheel of the cruiser and moved her sunglasses to the top of her head. She closed her eyes but soon her phone's ring pierced the silence.

"Hello," she said. "Yes, Cathy... The doctors just left and they couldn't give me anything definite on the corpse. Gail said it may be male... Sure, if you need clean-up help at the Swamp Donkey, I'll be on my way."

CHAPTER SIXTEEN

SATURDAY EVENING LARRY DID A FULL EXAMINATION of Ben's hotel room and his Jeep, but found nothing. Larry then returned to see Ben and questioned him about the night his father died. Ben told him every bit of detail he could remember.

Larry nodded. "So can you tell me more about this Pete?"

Ben didn't hesitate. "His last name was Buckingham. I remember because he used to tell us how he was related to the Royal Family and we believed him because he had such a strong British accent. We were just kids."

"Right. Grinder's camp that you told us about – completely torched."

"What! When?"

"The same night the pub blew up," Larry added.

"Holy shit," Ben replied. "Was Grinder at the pub when it blew up? Or the Trap House?"

"I'm not at liberty to discuss that; sorry."

"Last week," Ben continued after thinking a moment, "they told me to meet a redhead at the Lucky Strike parking lot. They said she'd be in a black '98 Intrepid, black bra on it. They gave me the code name *Galaxy* and said she'd reply with *Ruby*. Friday night they left a grey bin full of crystal meth by my mailbox."

Larry perked up. "And where is the meth now?"

Ben nodded. "I locked it up before I came in here. At the bus station in a guitar case and I nailed the locker key to a tree on the left-hand side of St. Bernard's church on Botsford."

Larry stood up.

"What's next?" Ben asked.

"We still can't hold you, but we'll have more questions once we have a chance to look into the information you gave us. You just stay put right here for the time being."

Twenty minutes later Larry arrived in Cathy's office with the guitar case, setting it on Cathy's desk and pulling the latch open. In it, they found the crystal meth, examined it, then Larry dialed a number on his phone. A few minutes later, a cop showed up and picked up the guitar case and its contents.

Cathy looked up at Larry and said. "Get some rest, you're going to need it."

Larry walked to his hotel room, dropped the change in his pockets in a bowl on the entry table and slipped off his shoes before pulling a bottle of Drambuie and Scotch whisky out of his two-bottle tote bag. He poured himself a healthy dram of each into a short tumbler, drinking the Rusty Nail on the rocks in one shot. He replenished the glass again, and then once more. Finally, he brought all of the pictures he could hold and spread them across one of the beds, scanning each one.

Just as he slipped under the covers and turned the light off, the phone rang.

"Hey, Larry," Chuck said. "Find the drugs?"

Larry sat up. "Yeah, a significant amount of meth stored at the bus station, which he was to drop off to a redhead in a 1998 Black Intrepid at the Lucky Strike bowling alley, but we haven't found anything on the redhead yet."

"Why don't you leave that with me? It'll be a thrill for my staff to figure out who she is."

At 7:00 a.m., Sunday morning, Larry showed up in the interview room, woke Ben up and told him about the skeleton they dug up in his shed.

"Just like I said," Ben stated solemnly, his eyes filling with water. "I'm hiding nothing, Larry. Told you about the drugs, too. Now do you believe the rest of the stuff I told you?"

"Did your father have a gold tooth?" asked the detective.

"Yeah," Ben replied, his voice taking on a down note.

"The belt fight you told us about..."

"Yeah?"

"Do you remember the buckle? We found one all rusted in the pit."

"Johnny Cash?" Ben said. Then he sat up straighter. "Yes, it was a Johnny Cash belt buckle."

"Stay put," Larry said. "I'll be back later."

Ben put his hands behind his neck and tilted his head back, trying to get the kinks out. He walked around the room, arms crossed, trying to figure out if he'd done the right thing by going to the cops with his story. Maybe Tony was right to avoid them at all costs, but he felt safe here.

A few hours later, Larry walked into the interview room with Diane and another cop in tow.

Diane walked straight to Ben and without a pause, said, "Benjamin Walsh. You're under arrest for the possession of narcotics for the purpose of trafficking, blackmail, extortion, and improperly interfering with human remains. You have the right to remain silent. Anything you say or do can be used against you in a court of law."

Then she slapped a page on the table and said. "You also have the right to retain and instruct counsel without delay. You also have the right to free and immediate legal advice from duty counsel by making free telephone calls to either Donna Dwelling during non-business hours or David

Brown during business hours. Their numbers are on the sheet. Do you understand?"

Ben caved in his chair and closed his eyes.

"Do you wish to call a lawyer?" Diane asked.

"Yes."

Larry added, "I wish to give you the following warning. You must clearly understand that anything said to you previously should not influence you or make you feel compelled to say anything at this time. Whatever you felt influenced or compelled to say earlier, you are not obliged to repeat, nor are you obliged to say anything further, but whatever you do say may be given as evidence. Do you understand?"

"Yes."

Larry continued. "Do you wish to say anything?"

"No."

After consenting to an oral swab, having been fingerprinted and processed for his arrest, Ben was moved to a meeting room and called a lawyer. He waited three hours alone in the room and he dozed off, his head cradled on one arm as he slumped over the table. Then the door swung open. Ben studied the newcomer – a dark-haired woman, maybe thirty, thirty-five, perched on high heels. She wore a black suit with white pinstripes and a crisp white blouse. She sat across from Ben, dropping her briefcase on the table – Ben jumped – then she put both hands on it as though she was going to pray with him.

"The name's Donna Dwelling," she said in a soft and measured voice as she stretched her arm for a handshake.

Ben stared at the cop standing at the door.

"Ben," she continued without moving anything but her lips, wrinkles not having yet crept up on her satin skin. "I'm here to represent you on a number of charges. First piece of advice: stop talking to the cops. Got it? Now Monday, tomorrow morning, you and I will be in court, before a judge, for a bail hearing. Do you have any questions?"

"No," Ben replied, his Adam's apple jumping up and down as he swallowed. He averted her eyes.

"Do you know what you are charged with, Ben?" she asked.

Ben nodded.

"You have to help me. Where were you Friday night?"

Ben closed his eyes and breathed out slowly.

"You see," she said. "Now that you've told them everything, they have you on kidnapping, narcotics, blackmail/extortion and interference with human remains. You've got to help me out here."

When Ben still didn't respond, his lawyer raised her voice. "Come on," she begged. "Let me help you. You're up to your eyeballs and they may have enough to keep you locked up forever. Now, can you tell me where you were Friday night?"

"Why couldn't I tell them everything? I've done nothing wrong. I'm innocent. I told them about being bullied into delivering the meth, and explained about Jack, and my dad."

"Where were you Friday night, Ben?"

"At home and then doing a delivery for the bastards."

"I'll see you at the bail hearing, Ben," Donna added as she closed the door behind her.

A few minutes later, Larry entered the room.

"You son of a bitch!" Ben snapped as he stood up. "I'm charged with a whole bunch of other shit now. Jesus Christ, Larry, I trusted you. How could you do this to me?"

"Remember, I didn't do any of this to you, Ben," Larry said softly. "I know it seems unfair, but the good news is that we ran you through our CPIC database and you came out clean. We just need more time to sort things out. About

Pete... I tracked him down. His name is Peter R. Buckingham and he lives in a special care facility in Sussex. He had his eyes scooped out of his head and his tongue chopped off back in the seventies. Someone found him on the side of the road, left for dead. He went crazy and was in psychiatric care up north for a good twenty years. The nurse I spoke to at the home said people around there were glad to see Pete – Thumbless Pete, to use her exact words – off of the streets. He was apparently a boisterous bum, a lost soul."

"What do you mean *Thumbless* Pete?" Ben asked.

"Thumbless, because he had only one thumb," Larry said. "Nobody knew much about him other than he came from overseas and was often hired as a handyman on farms around the area. And Ben, one more thing; if you're innocent, you wouldn't object to taking a lie detector test, would you?"

"I'll take a polygraph any day," Ben said, crossing his arms.

On Friday, February 28, Ben made page two of the newspaper.

> A Weldon man appeared in court this morning for a bail hearing after being charged with possession of narcotics, kidnapping, blackmail/extortion, and interference with human remains. Benjamin Walsh, 44, is charged with one count of possession of methamphetamine for the purpose of trafficking, kidnapping Jack Thibodeau and interference with the human remains of his father, Gerald Walsh.
>
> Walsh pleaded not guilty. He will be remanded in custody until he awaits his trial set before a Provincial Court on June 14. Acting on behalf of the accused was duty counsel Donna Dwelling with federal prosecutor Scott Livingstone arguing that the methamphetamine had a street value of more than $100,000.

CHAPTER SEVENTEEN

C HUCK, EYES WATERING FROM THE COLD, STOOD shivering in front of City Hall as the Arctic air made its way under his trench coat.

The day before, he'd asked two of his employees, Matt King and Sarah Long, to focus on getting him a list of 1998 black Intrepid owners within a thirty-kilometre radius. There were eighteen. Chuck then put Paula to the task of deciphering which one was most likely to be the bad apple. By the end of the day, one name and only one name remained at the top.

Chuck stepped out into the bright February morning light and paced alongside the overhang of the building, waiting for Service New Brunswick's offices to open. He watched as the concierge hit massive icicles hanging along the eaves of the building with the long handle of a rake. The gigantic spikes broke loose and crashed to the ground.

Catherine, short of seasoned investigators, had begged Chuck to assist them earlier in the week, offering to hire him on full-time. Chuck had taken a few days to make the decision, pulled between his business and the excitement of this case. He officially went on leave from Hanley's Investigations, and when he accepted, Catherine jumped for joy.

"You know, Chuck," Cathy said as she finished filing out the papers to begin his employment, "I've heard several stories about you. All quite colourful, especially the one where you went undercover as a Mr. Smith. I'd love to hear your version."

Chuck was much thinner then with long hair and a beard. It was the eighties and Chuck, a.k.a. Barnie Smith, was working undercover in the largest manhunt Atlantic Canada had ever seen. It was fall and he dressed in camouflage, heading in the deep woods where Craig Hudson, a serial killer who later confessed to murdering six women, was thought to be hiding. For almost a week, Chuck slipped through the evergreens, his hands thick and gooey with black spruce resin, sniffing around cabins and bogs pretending to hunt. He knew he was on the home stretch when one morning, after a restless, pitch-black night in a crow's nest, he watched quietly as the outlaw, rifle in hand, parked himself underneath Chuck's nest to void his bowels. A few hours later, paramedics walked out of the swamps with the "Most Wanted" on a stretcher, a bullet hole through the top of his head.

Chuck grabbed the picture of the redhead from his pocket and held it up, curling it inward in his right hand as if playing Blackjack. At that instant, the fair-skinned girl in the picture walked up the steps to City Hall and they shared a glance when he held the door open for her. Chuck smiled to himself. He could be on to something. Following the swing of her coat to the jam-packed elevator, he found a spot in the corner next to her, catching a whiff of her perfume and perhaps a hint of cucumber from her stack of stiff red hair. When she got off on the eighth floor, he tagged along down an endless corridor. At the end of the hall, she opened a glass door to the Town Registry office, and when she noticed he was right behind her, she held the door open.

"My turn," she said.

"Thank you," he replied.

Inside the office, he stood first in line, watching as she hung her coat up and took ownership of a cash register in a booth alongside five others. He noticed the swiftness of her long fingers tapping at the cash. She was quite pretty and the redness on her cheeks was still there when he stood in front of her. The name "Jody" was displayed on a gold label pinned to her dress.

"Good morning, sir," she said with a wide smile. "How can I help you this morning?"

"I'm here about my frigging property tax!" he shouted. "I'm paying way too much for the damn thing and I want to talk to somebody right now. I don't own a goddamn football field! All I have is a small little home outside of town. This is highway robbery and I want to talk to somebody... NOW!"

Within a few minutes, Chuck sat in an office behind closed doors with a property assessor.

"I want to talk to the big boss," he stated. "I've talked to you idiots before and nothing ever changed."

Minutes later, he sat in the director's office and told him the reason for his visit. Chuck wanted information on his employee Jody.

"She's been here for less than a year," the employer noted. "She's an excellent worker. Smart too. I don't know what else to tell you except that her last name is Tupper."

"We have reason to believe that she may be involved in criminal activity," Chuck explained. "You're no fool. You know criminals send their puppets to take jobs like these for intel and use it to their advantage. Jody is probably here to get access to driver licenses and car registrations. I've been in the business long enough to know that brand new four-wheelers and motorcycles disappear the same day they're registered. That's no fluke."

The director sat there, slack-jawed.

Chuck continued. "I need you to keep this quiet and give me her address and any surveillance tapes on the cash register in front of her."

"Let me find her address," the director answered without hesitation as he walked over to a file cabinet and pulled out a labelled manila folder. "Unfortunately, the cameras don't work. They haven't for months. We just didn't get the funding, but they act as a deterrent. Here's her address."

"What does she drive?"

"Let me see," he said as he clicked a few keys on the computer. "A 1998 Intrepid. Black."

Chuck pretended to be still upset when he walked by Jody on his way out. He checked her address and then met Cathy and Larry at a corner booth at the cops' mess hall in the neighboring town of Dieppe.

At 2:30 p.m., Tuesday, February 25, Diane, surrounded by filing cabinets, sighed at the reports on her desk, wondering if she'd made the right move. She'd studied physics at UNB, but was becoming restless and had joined Ground Search and Rescue, mostly to be with her boyfriend at the time. But even after he was history later that summer, she stayed on. By the next year she had graduated from the Regina Depot, then worked three years in Northern Ontario as a patrol officer. Initially she was excited to be transferred to Moncton – finally close to home again – but the restlessness returned. She'd had enough of patrolling the streets and wanted to do serious investigative work. Well, she got what she wanted, and then some. She wadded a piece of paper into a ball as a call came in. Cradling the phone between her ear and shoulder, she listened.

"Tina," Robert Snide, a constable working the RCMP detachment's front door stated. "Tina Walsh, a cook at Don's Diner, hasn't showed up for work for two days. The owner, Adam Richards, called us yesterday but we told him, of course, we don't check out missing adults for twenty-four hours," Robert continued. "But he insisted that she only missed one day's work in twelve years. And even then, he said she called to let him know. He's been calling her apartment, but there's still no answer. I just finished filling out a missing person report."

"And?" Diane grumbled, fighting a wave of tiredness. "What do you want from me?"

"Well, in the report... he only knows of one relative."

"I don't have all day."

"Her name's Tina Walsh," he explained. "He said she has a brother named Ben. Figured she might be related to..."

"I'll be right down!"

Once downstairs, Diane peeked through the little window in the door leading to the lobby and spotted a short, older man sitting, his foot tapping restlessly.

"Mr. Richards? You're here about Tina?"

"Yes. She hasn't shown up for work and I've been to her apartment but there's no answer," he said, obviously worried. "That's two days she's missed. That's not like her."

"What's her last name, sir?" Diane asked as she wrote down the information.

"Walsh," the restaurant owner replied in a hurried pace. "She's single and I don't think she was ever married. She lives alone with her dog... uh, Blackie... at 359 Robinson Street."

"Did you drop by her place, knock on the door?"

Mr. Richards only shook his head quickly while wringing his hands.

Half an hour later, after informing Larry of her plans, Diane and another constable, Guy Paleske, knocked at Tina's door on Robinson. No answer, but a dog barked. Fifteen minutes later, after tracking down the landlord, the door opened to a dim kitchen area and a fifty-pound Sheprador, tail wagging, jumped on Diane's leg. The bachelor apartment smelled of dog pee and cigarette smoke and they held their noses as they searched through the rest of the apartment. The place was filthy with a pile of dirty dishes in the sink, an overflowing kitchen garbage can and stacks of old magazines on the counter next to open cereal boxes. Diane opened the pale, drab-coloured curtains in the living room and found a fogged and dirty window behind them. The floor was cluttered with clothes and the unmade bed was littered with a trail of tissues.

"Larry?" Diane asked once the phone picked up. "We're at Tina Walsh's apartment and she's not here. We found a dog, a quite hungry dog, and the place is disgusting."

"You guys stay there and guard the place," Larry responded. "I'm sending a forensic team ASAP."

"Uh, what about the dog?" Diane said, looking down at Blackie, who had settled by her feet.

"Right. Can you take it to the SPCA?"

Blackie looked up at Diane. She was half tempted to take him home.

"How you feeling, Chuck?" Cathy asked.

"Who? Me? Never been better."

"The scars on the side of your face are healing nicely," Larry said.

"Sharon doesn't think so," he added. "She doesn't want me to work at all."

Cathy briefly put her hand on Chuck's. "Are you still seeing the doctor?"

Chuck didn't hesitate. "No. No need to. I got a clean bill of health last time I was in."

Cathy shook her head. "You were lucky, Chuck. Did anyone find out what happened exactly?"

Chuck shrugged. "All I got is that the other driver ran a red light. Probably an accident, right?"

The table was silent for a moment, then Cathy took the last bite of her chicken wrap and wiped her mouth. Quietly, she said, "By the way, Jack Thibodeau's parents stopped by this morning to offer their help. And we still haven't found Tina."

"I found the owner of the Intrepid though," Chuck added. "Her name's Jody Tupper and she lives in a new house on Palisade Avenue, Number 105. She's running a sophisticated grow-op. Most of her plants are mature with only a few seedlings. Get yourself a warrant, if you know what I mean. Look at these shots of the plants."

"Hold on, Chuck," Cathy said. "That's called

trespassing... Oh, forget it!" She sighed. "Keep going."

"There are over a hundred pot plants in the basement, I'm not joking, and I'd say it's harvest time soon," he added in a relaxed manner as he handed her the digital camera.

Cathy squinted as she moved from one picture to the next. "Thousand bucks per plant... that's a heck of a lot of cash. I'll put the house on surveillance while we get a search warrant. Send me those shots please. Oh – any signs of anyone else living in the house?"

"I'm getting to that. And, I'm disappointed that I didn't find a goalie's mask in there. Thought they may be related... But, I did find a few pictures of her with men near a Storky's Waste Remediation truck. That's somethin'."

Cathy grinned. "You never know what you'll find in this business. There's a meeting at three this afternoon, a discovery of sorts. Please show up and be ready to present what you have on her."

By mid-afternoon, the large meeting room at the RCMP detachment filled with a flurry of yellow-stripes and experts. From the podium, several of them took turns projecting slides and presenting their findings. The RCMP Arson Investigator described the ingredients used in both the Swamp Donkey and camp blasts as C4 (Composition Four) plastic explosives, and a representative from the Criminal Intelligence Service talked about the gang's drug imprint on the area. Then, a member of Atlantic Canada's Drug Unit reported its findings on the residue found at the meth lab in the back property of the camp.

"I would describe it as a super lab," he added. "We found gas masks, digital scales, portable stoves, funnels and other paraphernalia and the place was guarded, as one of our team found out, by bear traps hidden beneath leaves. A Health Canada chemist confirmed the existence of the toxic ingredients – anhydrous ammonia, paint thinner, metallic lithium, hydrochloric or sulphuric acids, starter fluid, and camping fuel – in the ten-litre vats of liquid that were bubbling on industrial-sized hot plates. These ingredients were also found on the walls, ceilings and in the drains."

Another expert noted that surveillance on Jody Tupper's every movement was underway. And then, Dr. Karen Watson, intense in her high-spirited way, stood up and matter-of-factly showed the skeletal remains of Gerald Walsh on the projector screen, taking away any ambiguity about the fact that they were at least thirty years old. She relayed details of the forensic dig and confirmed it to belong to a male, 5' 11" with broken ribs and a fractured hyoid bone – her conclusion, death by strangulation. "Forensic anthropologist Dr. John Taylor and I have determined with 99% accuracy that the corpse is that of Gerald "Gerry" Walsh whose son, Benjamin Walsh, you have in custody. Several techniques were used to identify the body, including a three-dimensional facial reconstruction that was compared to a picture of the deceased. In addition, his wallet and a belt buckle were retrieved from the site which also helped us confirm his identity."

She paused, displaying other slides, this time of Jack Thibodeau's family.

"Based on work performed by pathologist Dr. Gail Patrick, the three adults in this family died as a result of stab wounds, while the baby was suffocated," she said. "They were in a rigor mortis state when they were found, but rigor mortis begins at the lower jaw and neck and spreads downward. In these homicides, only the jaws were rigid, which puts the time of death at less than five hours before they were discovered at the crime scene. As for the bodies recovered from the blast at the pub, they were all identified. All of the deceased died from the impact of the blast."

Chuck took his turn and displayed a few pictures: one of Jody with a man; the other of the same couple with another couple in front of a truck labelled Storky's Waste Remediation Inc.

"This girl," he stated, "according to our suspect Benjamin Walsh, was a delivery girl. And although the delivery never happened, Ben told us he was to meet with her in the Lucky Strike bowling alley parking lot to drop off a package. She lived in Montreal all of her life and now we find her working at the Registry Office here in town as a clerk, staying in a heck of a nice place."

Larry then took to the podium and showed a picture of the goalie mask.

"According to Chuck," Larry said, "Jack Thibodeau hired him as a PI and described the mask wore by his captor as one worn by Gary Bromley when he played for the Vancouver Canucks. We're currently checking its manufacturer. The drug found in Ben's guitar case is crystal meth, the same drug cooked at the camp. We also found hashish in his dirty laundry, in a pair of jeans. And although we know Ben's father died from strangulation, we're having doubts about the killer since Ben told us that the murder – in 1971 – was committed by his father's friend "Thumbless Pete" and Ben's brother Tony. Pete apparently forced the boys to bury the father in a barn on Ben's property, in the ground below the floorboards."

Catherine also noted that Tina Walsh's disappearance was linked to her brother, Ben Walsh, and that he had been notified of the additional charge. She wrapped the session by assigning various tasks to officers, including those required by Larry and Chuck, and opened the floor for questions. A half hour later, she thanked everyone for working so conscientiously on the case and called it a day.

CHAPTER EIGHTEEN

CHUCK CUPPED HIS BODY AGAINST SHARON WHILE she slept, listening to the mild March winds rustle through the maples in the backyard. The snow on the roof was melting and gurgling down the gutters. It all made a bit of a racket, but she was not an early bird and no wind would wake her until she was good and ready.

He also heard seagulls wailing and he made a mental list of things to do around the house once up – put shovels away, wash the cars, hang bird-feeders and sweep the salt and sand from the driveway.

The phone rang.

"Come on, Chuck," she said, stirring awake, holding on to his arm as he tried to move away. "It's Sunday. Let it ring."

"Might be your mother!" he said, laughing as he reached for the phone. Once he hung up, he looked over at Sharon. Her eyelids were gently closed. He paused. Next minute, he eased out of bed and got dressed quietly and closed the bedroom door, knowing exactly how to pull it to avoid the squeak.

Chuck stepped outside and into the bright, early-morning sun, letting the crisp air into his lungs. The snow on the front lawn was receding and patches of grass had emerged. *There'll be more freezing rain and more snow on the way*, the radio declared. Well, now that's good news, Chuck thought. March is coming in like a lion.

By ten o'clock, he sat comparing notes with Cathy and

Larry at the detachment when Diane stuck her head in the office, a wide grin on her face.

"Can I come in?" Diane asked.

Cathy nodded, "Yes, what is it?"

"You'll never guess what, guys," she said cheerfully. "Ben and Tony are twins!"

Catherine's eyes widened. "What?"

"I just figured it out," she said proudly. "I got a fax from the Department of National Defence on Tony and found out that both Ben and Tony were born on February fourteen, 1958!"

"Well, I'll be damned," Larry said, elbowing Chuck. "Valentine twins. And of course that means Tony and Ben have the same freakin' DNA."

Chuck put his head down and concentrated, trying to figure out how the news could change the investigation on Ben. "Same DNA, but not necessarily the same prints... right? Anyone?"

Larry cleared his throat. "For all we know, they might be both in on it."

Diane rustled the papers in her hands and continued. "I have more...listen to this. The mask was custom-made in Petawawa, Ontario by a retired army officer. Only a few dozen were made around this time last year. I called the maker, but there was no answer. I left a voicemail."

"Well, since Ben told me he got it for his birthday last year," Larry said, "the maker should be able to narrow it down to a short list of buyers within a two to four week period."

"I'm on it," said Diane. "I'll check Tony's prints. DND has them and said the prints would be faxed within an hour."

"Also get me Tony's home address, Diane," Cathy said.

"Will do that too," Diane shouted on as she let herself out the door.

"What about Ben's prints?" Larry asked.

Cathy replied, "Still no match anywhere except for the glass found at his sister's apartment."

An hour later, Diane returned to Cathy's office with Don Foster and Denis Whalen.

"Well this must be good news," Cathy said. "The whole forensic department is here."

"The fingerprints on the glass are a close match to Ben's," Don said with a smile. "But not exactly. There's a slight difference in the minutia. Mr. Tony Walsh is your boy. His prints also match those we found at the Thibodeau residence."

Larry thought a moment, then asked Don, "Can I see a picture of the drinking glass?"

Don nodded. "I'll be right back." Moments later, he handed Larry a photo.

"I knew it," Larry said as he stared at the picture of the drinking glass. "This glass was taken from Ben's house... unless his sister had the same drinking glasses. So... Tony tried to frame Ben? Why?"

"Do you have a street address for Tony yet?" Chuck asked of Diane.

"I'm getting there. I'll be right back."

Larry stood and grabbed his things. "I'm going to have a talk with Ben. Meet back here in an hour."

Ben's neck was as stiff as the iron bars on his lock-up cell window. After being escorted by an armed guard who stayed behind Ben's steel cell door, Larry found Ben lying on a creaky mattress, hunched beneath a light blanket, his back to him.

"Ben," Larry said while removing photos from an envelope. "I have a few pictures to show you. It's the girl, Jody, and her boyfriend. This is the girl you were supposed to deliver drugs to at the bowling alley. Please, look at these and tell me if you recognize either one of them."

Ben didn't budge. "Go to hell, Larry."

Larry raised his voice. "You never told me you and

Tony were twins, Ben."

"Why do you care? You put me here."

"I didn't put you here. You had the drugs. Listen, I'm not out to get you. We have reasons to believe that you're innocent and that your brother may be behind this whole affair."

Ben threw the blanket off and jumped up. He felt dizzy and sat down on the bed, rubbing his hands over his face.

"You look awful, Ben," Larry noted as Ben stared at him with sunken cheeks. "Have you been eating anything?"

Ben stared stonily ahead. He raked his fingers through is hair and rubbed his beard. "What's with Tony?"

"The fingerprints in your sister's apartment are Tony's and we think the glass came from your kitchen."

Ben stood, stifling the urge to scream. "Huh! Tony's print on my glass?"

Larry scratched his head. "Yes. Can you tell me the last time you saw him?"

Ben stretched his arms over his head and rested his hands against the cement wall. "I'm dying in here, Larry, and what are you doing to get me out?"

"I promise you that I'll do everything in my power to get you out. You have my word. Please. Sit down. Talk to me."

Ben leaned his back against the wall and stared at the floor. He took a breath through his nostrils, bent in half and touched the tip of his boots. He straightened up and took two steps forward, putting both hands on the sink, becoming increasingly aware of the cold steel, the hollow pipes and the grey cement wall in front of him. Without turning, he asked. "Can you get me a cell with a window? And cigarettes?"

Larry called out to the prison guard stationed at the door and asked for smokes and a light. A few moments later, the guard handed Larry a half-empty pack of Export A and a lighter through the slot in the door. Larry returned to his chair and Ben returned to his bed. "Here. Smoke. I'll get you a room with a view before the end of the week."

Ben lit up a cigarette, took a deep drag on it, his body responding to the smoke like a warm blanket wrapped around his lungs "Thank you. Can you please make sure I never run out of these while I'm in here?"

"You've got my word. Now, Tony."

"I saw him a couple of days after my birthday. We had a few drinks and crashed at the Fox motel on Elmwood Drive."

"When is your birthday?"

"Valentine's Day."

"Are you close to him?"

Ben looked bewildered for a moment, shook his head and took a long pause before he spoke. "Not really."

"You ever been?"

"Close? When we were kids, I guess. He joined the army at eighteen and we only ever heard from him on postcards. A few years ago, he moved back east and we've talked a few times but he never gave me his telephone number. And Tina never gave me hers either. Some family I have."

"Did you tell him what you told us?"

"You mean about Jack and Grinder? Yeah, I told him everything that was going on in my life."

"Ben," Larry continued. "We also found an old toolbox with your father's remains." Ben's eyes widened. "In it, we found all sorts of things that you may be able to explain, and we also found a fair amount of animal bones scattered here and there in the barn."

Larry handed pictures of the box's content to Ben. He lobbed a silent *I-can't-believe-it* expression to Larry. "I remember this stuff, these *Amazing Spider-Man* comics. I never knew where they disappeared to."

"Can you tell me more about Tony? What was he like growing up?"

"A gun fanatic," Ben said, his eyes turning downward. "I think that's why he joined the army. He spent a lot of time in that old horse-barn after Dad was... gone... and he never let Tina or me near the place."

Under the surface of his consciousness, Ben plowed back through the years to his father's burial and Tony's departure for the army, but he couldn't recall a whole lot in between. Maybe he didn't want to remember. He threw his back against the cot and stared at the ceiling, one foot resting on the other.

"He loved knives, too. He had a collection of them. The neighbours had a cat and I remember him, yeah, hanging it by the neck in the old horse-barn. The cat gagged and kicked... and while it was still alive, Tony opened up its guts. Said he wanted to know if cats really had nine lives. He punctured the poor animal over and over, blood pissing everywhere. He cut his head off and threw it down the floor and when it dried up, he hung it up as a trophy. He'd pick at it, scraping the fur off, just like he did with rabbits and frogs. The poor things covered the barn walls. But, then he got a padlock and that put an end to our visits, Tina and I."

Larry nodded. "Go on."

Ben stared at the ceiling, his hands tucked under his head. "Tony changed a lot after Dad died. Lived in his head mostly and he hated Mom for letting it all happen. Even the postcards he'd sent were addressed to me, not to her."

"I really need you to work with me on this, Ben."

"You bet," Ben added with a nod. "Give me a window and smokes and, of course, get me out of here, Larry."

Larry hurried out of the city lock-up cell and stopped at the desk where Diane, typing quickly, had her eyes glued to the screen.

"Did you find anything about Tony yet?" Larry stood in front of her, one elbow resting on top of her filing cabinet. "We need his alibi for Friday, February twenty-second. Where the hell was he that day?"

Diane stopped typing, grabbed her notepad. "I have

all the information you need," she said, grinning. "Let's get Chuck on the phone if he's not here. You're going to like this Larry. Follow me."

The two of them gathered in Cathy's office and Chuck arrived a few minutes later.

"Tony Walsh was married to Susan Armstrong in 1978, and by 1983 had three kids," Diane said in one breath following the notes in her black notebook. "His wife put a peace bond on him after their divorce in '98. She still lives in Petawawa and remarried in 1999. That's when he moved back here. Career wise, in 1975 he joined the Princess Patricia Canadian Light Infantry or PPCLI and was posted in Winnipeg. As a private, he toured six months in Cyprus and conducted exercises in Germany until the eighties. Part of the Brigade in Germany was off and on for Reforger Bataillon in Winnipeg."

"He got around," Chuck noted.

Diane flipped a page of her top-spiral notebook. "Then, during the eighties, the exercises were out west and, now Master Corporal Tony Walsh, he was stationed in Petawawa with the airborne regiment. After a couple of years there, he was promoted to sergeant. He did some tours in Bosnia and Rwanda in peacekeeping missions. In the nineties, he served in the First Gulf War as a sharp shooter. For about four to five years during the same period, he was also part of the JTF and was stationed in Dwyer Hill, Ontario. In 1999, he became a warrant officer in the school, or what they call the Infantry Combat Centre in Gagetown, so finally back here in his native New Brunswick. He was honoured several times for his sharp-shooting skills, but he turned to alcohol around 2001, it seems, and was kicked out. He is now unemployed, drives a Saturn wagon, and lives at 191 Tower Woods Road, north of Marysville."

Cathy nodded appreciatively. "So, this guy is no amateur."

"I just came back from talking to Ben," Larry said. "He had complained about the gang to Tony right after his birthday. Even told him about Jack."

Everyone sat still, waiting as Cathy debated what to do next.

"This is a tough one guys," she said. "You can talk to him, but without any warrants or solid proof, you can't arrest him or read him his rights yet. Let me get in touch with Scott Livingstone and get the ball rolling on warrants."

"What do you mean no proof?" Chuck exclaimed. "We've got his print on the glass."

"I know," Cathy replied. "But that's not enough. Let's take it slow. Understand, guys?"

"While we wait," Larry suggested quietly, "let Chuck and I pay him a social visit. No harm, right?" He shrugged. "If he's not home, we'll peek around the property."

"You are not peeking around this guy's property." Cathy lifted her index and pointed at Chuck. "That's a no... but if the two of you want to talk it over and come back with a strategy I can approve, then go to it. Otherwise, don't waste my time."

"Yes ma'am," Larry replied. Chuck nodded.

Half an hour later, Chuck and Larry returned to Cathy's office. Larry outlined the plan, saying they wouldn't do anything but talk to Tony about Ben and Tina. If Tony wasn't home, they'd walk away. "You know me, Cathy. I wouldn't be doing this if I thought it wasn't the right thing to do."

Cathy took off her reading glasses, looking tired, and rubbed the bridge of her nose. "If I decide to approve it, you will do it my way... four officers of the Fredericton detachment's tactical team will escort you there and back and be on stand-by near the road. That also means keeping your radio on at all times, no exception. Diane is on the phone right now with the director of municipal affairs in that region to get a picture of what the roads in an out of the property look like and, more importantly, what his property looks like. Once I understand the logistics to my satisfaction, I'll give you an answer."

CHAPTER NINETEEN

A T 10:30 A.M., MONDAY, MARCH 3, AFTER TWO hours of driving, Larry and Chuck reached Tower Woods Road and parked on the side of the route, behind a car covered in snow.

When Chuck and Larry got out of their vehicle, so did the four uniformed officers. Chuck spun and set his gaze from one officer to the other. He touched the brim of his hat and said: "Gentlemen."

The officers, ready for action, nodded. The oldest officer straightened his back and said, "We'll be right here."

At this point, neither Larry or Chuck could see the single snowblower swipe leading to house number 191, at least not until they'd walked past the six-foot-high, die-hard snow banks.

As Larry and Chuck moved down the crunchy, four hundred-yard path, Chuck in the lead and both carrying a 9mm semi-automatic pistol and a radio, they surveyed what they'd memorized of the property the day before: the driveway straight as dry lasagna, the farmhouse and a leafless apple orchard on the flag lot, a small shed tucked behind the house, and a huge barn in front of unharvested land.

Now close to the house, its shingles tortured by years of neglect, they were greeted by rotting stairs and shrink-wrapped windows. Smoke flowed out of the tall, narrow chimney and a large stack of firewood, the larger pieces split with an axe, stood in a small open shed next to the house. Foot prints, speckled with woodchips, started at the side door and circled around the corner of the house towards the back. Larry knocked on a scratched and blistered white wooden door, and though they knew what to expect, they were both stunned when a clone of Ben appeared. The twin had a crew cut.

"Morning," Tony said, looking at them with bloodshot eyes. "Who are you?"

"Are you Tony Walsh?" Chuck asked.

"Yes, I am. Who wants to know?"

"We do," Chuck continued. "I'm Detective Hanley and he's Detective White. We'd like to talk to you about your brother Ben."

Scratching his head as he talked, Tony said, "Ben! What's he done?"

Chuck walked up the steps, hitting his feet against each other to get rid of the snow. "Mind if we come in?"

Tony swung the door open, inviting them into a run-down, grey kitchen – grimy floors, dirty dishes, garbage bags stacked in a corner, and empty liquor bottles everywhere. The scuffed, peeling linoleum had long lost its appeal and worn-down plywood peeked through the beat-up floor. A chill hung in the kitchen. A pile of firewood sat on a newspaper next to a wood stove and Tony offered them a seat at a filthy rectangular table next to the kitchen window. Behind them, a sofa, still opened into a bed, took up half of the kitchen living space. The archway leading to the remainder of the house was boarded up with plywood.

Tony detected their curiosity. "I can't afford to heat up the whole house. It's over a hundred years old and the insulation is paper thin."

"How long have you been living here?" Chuck asked.

Tony crossed his arms. "Thought you were here to talk about Ben? What did he do?"

"Do you have a TV? Radio? Internet? You've probably seen it all over the news if you do," Larry replied. "No? We're investigating an explosion in the Moncton area, the same night that a family of four was killed in their home. And,

I don't know if you're aware of this, but your sister Tina is missing. We think that maybe Ben has something to do with it, so we have him in custody. When's the last time you saw Ben or Tina?"

Chuck, facing the back kitchen window, noticed a shed with smoke coming out of its stovepipe. Before Tony had a chance to answer Larry, Chuck spoke. "What do you have cooking in the back yard?"

"Really?" Tony replied with a sneer. "You here to question me or talk about Ben? The people that owned this place had a bomb shelter in the back with a wood stove in it. Guess they were worried about the end of the world. I do some woodworking in there. That's where I keep all my tools and it's easier to heat. Now where were we about Ben and Tina?"

"When's the last time you either saw or talked to them?" Larry asked again.

Rubbing his hand across his jaw, he said. "I can't remember the last time I saw either one. It's been a long time. We're not close."

Itching his nose, Chuck asked. "What's cooking on the stove? Smells like pork roast."

"Yeah... that's it," he replied, stone-faced. "Pork roast! Well if we're done here, I'd like to get back to what I was doing."

On their way to the car, Larry pinched his nose. "What a stench in there."

"Can you believe that cock and bull story about the bomb shelter?" Chuck asked.

"I don't believe a word that came out of his mouth. If he's trying to save on wood, why does he keep two fires going? That path going to the shelter was dug out since the last snow. Lots of woodchips, trail's practically brown. He's keeping it open for something and I don't think it's for woodworking."

Chuck added in a serious tone. "He totally creeped me out. Something really doesn't smell right." Once out of sight of the house, Chuck stopped, pulled an empty beer bottle from his trench coat pocket, along with a box of wooden matches from another pocket. He smiled widely. "Let's double-check some prints on this guy. Give me a couple of plastic bags, Larry. Best make sure we've got the right person before we send in the troops."

"You're a genius, Chuck."

At nine o'clock sharp the next morning, March 4, Larry and Constable Brian Stairs sat in Judge Arthur Thériault's office's waiting area eager to present their case and obtain a search warrant on Tony Walsh.

"What's this judge like?" Larry asked. "Do you think he'll go for both warrants?"

"He's a tough nut to crack," Brian replied. "But I wouldn't be here if I didn't think we had a chance. With Tony's prints matching those at the Thibodeau residence and on Tina's glass, I think he might go for it."

Judge Thériault, a balding man in his 60's, sat across the two of them in his chamber, listening to Larry as he outlined his reasons.

"I've reviewed the attachments to the information to obtain and conclude from all of this evidence that a warrant for the search and seizure of Tony Walsh's property, located at 191 Tower Woods Road, be issued," the judge said. "The bond is set at $750,000."

By early afternoon, Diane, along with two police officers, Rob Shrew and Kevin Colt from the nearby RCMP detachment in Fredericton, stood at the door at 191 Tower Woods Road with the warrant in hand. Larry and Chuck waited at the bottom of the steps. There was no answer, no sign of smoke in the chimney either and the Saturn wagon was gone. Police officers forced their way into the locked door and within half an hour a truck geared with a front plow opened the long driveway to the farmhouse.

They all walked in, except for Larry and Chuck, who headed straight to the back yard where they used a pry bar to unlatch the underground bomb shelter's locked door.

In the meantime, Kevin unscrewed a plywood sheet from the far end wall of the kitchen and the living room opened up. Diane, with her duty flashlight in an overhand grip, as if ready to stab someone, scanned the area. She took a few steps back as her cone of light showed two skeletons, the corpses almost devoid of skin, sitting on the couch. Their lip-less mouths hung open. The smell drove her out of the house.

Larry pulled a short string and the light came on behind the steel door. They stood back as a vile, slightly metallic smell hit their noses. Chuck unbuttoned the top of his shirt and covered his mouth with one of his gloves. As they moved down the steep and narrow concrete stairs, a cadaver came into view, resting against a wall of the dirt cellar floor. The deceased was a fully dressed, but headless woman, whose white uniform, labelled Don's Diner, was drenched in blood. The pair stepped outside as Diane zipped out of the house, her face as pale as the snow she stepped on.

"Diane. What did you find?" Larry asked, shaking his head.

"There are two skeletons in the living room. What about you? What's in there?" she asked with trepidation.

"We've got a fresh one."

Larry called Cathy from his cell phone, telling her about the discoveries.

"Any sign of Tony?" Cathy asked in her usual managerial way.

"Of course not," Larry replied. "Call forensics right away and tell them to bring at least three body bags. I think we may have found Tina."

"No car, Larry?" she said.

"His car's gone."

"I'll put a trace on it right away and let the military police in Gagetown know as well."

Rob and Kevin came out of the house. Rob, having quit smoking for well over a year, lifted his index and middle fingers towards his mouth. Kevin handed him a cigarette and, as Rob exhaled, he noticed footprints on a path alongside a fence. He followed in the footsteps until he noticed a pot hanging on a fence post.

"Guys!" he shouted. "Come look at this."

Chuck walked over and put his camera to his eyes. The viewfinder revealed a head of white hair, mixed in with browning blood, in the open container.

On the drive back to Moncton, Larry called to confirm that the woman had to be Tina.

Cathy spoke. "Larry, Tony's Saturn was found on the highway near Grand Falls at noon, a two-hour drive north of his house. The goalie mask was in the trunk, but no weapons. There is no sign of Tony either, but all detachments across the province are on high alert. I need a picture of Tony for the media. Are you far from his house?"

"We left about twenty minutes ago," Larry answered. "But if you need a picture of the bastard, we'll go back."

Chuck raised his eyebrows as he pulled a photo from his trench coat. "No worries; I just happen to have one. I've got one of him in his army gear, picked it off the wall. We'll stop and fax it from the nearest detachment."

Larry shook his head. "Did you hear that, Cathy? I've got Inspector Clouseau with me."

At noon, Diane pulled up at the Fredericton RCMP detachment. It'd stormed the night before over much of the city and plows were pushing the snow in the corners of the parking lot. Her hands were shaking. She steadied them against the wheel for a moment, got out and walked in.

"Diane," Larry said as they waited for Chuck to finish sending the picture to Cathy. "They found the mask in Tony's car."

"What a coincidence," Diane said. "I just got a call from the mask's creator and he remembers designing two for Tony Walsh last year around this time. They were friends from the army and he sketched initials inside – TW and BW. Tony asked for that specifically."

Once in the office, they dialled Cathy who congratulated them all for a job well done.

"Since you guys left," she informed them, "they've cordoned off Tony's property and forensics are taking samples. Don and Denis are on their way, as well as John Taylor and Karen Watson. Oh, and Gail Patrick, too. They'll be at it all night, I'm sure. All RCMP detachments in the country and police departments in Maine are on the lookout. The hunt is on, everyone, and the story will be aired tonight on local and national news."

The next morning, March 5, every newspaper's main focus was on the madman. Tony's picture beamed on television sets across the nation.

CHAPTER TWENTY

TONY, DRESSED IN COVERALLS AND CARRYING A HEAVY hockey bag, climbed up Roy Marone's eighteen-wheeler. Sitting straight, he smiled at the driver as though he'd known him for years. Marone jacked up the heat as the truck picked up speed heading for the American border.

"Sure appreciate you stopping," Tony said, rubbing his arms. "Not a lot of people pick up hikers anymore."

"I never get tired of the company," Roy said while he sucked back an extra-large Tim Horton's coffee. "Gets pretty boring sometimes."

"Where you heading?"

"A long haul to Atlanta, Georgia and Charlotte, North Carolina. But thank God I get to see a race."

"A race?"

"Yep," he replied. "NASCAR in North Carolina."

"What's in the back?"

"A load of paper... enough to write from here to eternity."

By late afternoon, the semi pulled into a rest area off Interstate 95 in Maine and by the break of dawn the next morning, Tony, behind the semi's wheel, headed back to Canada alone. Half an hour before hitting the border in Calais, Maine, he pulled into a car dealership and asked to test drive a Jeep Cherokee, leaving behind Roy Marone's ID and truck. Half a kilometre from the Canadian border, he parked the vehicle near a culvert, setting through the woods on foot. Hours later, while a delivery man on Canadian soil was busy with a customer, Tony hopped in the back of his courier delivery truck and hid.

"March sixth," Cathy said without expecting an answer from Larry, Chuck or Diane as she flipped through the calendar on her desk. "Tony Walsh has been busy. We have his prints in Maine where he killed a trucker, left his truck while test driving a Jeep and jumped the border through the woods yesterday morning. Border security has him on tape. Then, across the border, we have his prints on a delivery truck he stole. The truck was found last night in Sussex."

Chuck sucked air between his teeth.

Cathy turned toward Chuck. "I have a job for you. I want you to go undercover. If you're up to the challenge, of course."

Chuck stood, intrigued. "Now we're talking."

"I've got it all figured out," Cathy continued. "I have an uncle in Riverside-Albert... a minister. I'll call him and see if you can board at his house for a while. You good with that?"

Chuck smiled. "I could be persuaded."

Then Diane spoke up. "The military police will be coming in later today to discuss what we have on Tony and see how we can work together. They don't have anything to do with him because he's no longer in the army, but they're cooperative and will give us any information we need."

"What are we doing with Ben?" Larry asked.

"He's being released as we speak," Cathy noted. "We dropped all pending charges."

"Even kidnapping Jack?" Larry asked. "What about the drug charges?"

"We're not going to get a statement from Jack, and Ben was under duress," she continued. "The Commissioner and I are of the same opinion that Ben is clean. The Walsh boys would have been very young when their father's homicide took place, and Pete is in no position to be tried or even interviewed; we're already been down that road. We both agree that the gang was manufacturing meth and using Ben as a delivery boy. There is simply no one to hang the responsibility on at this point, though the file will be officially kept open until we're satisfied we've done all we can here. Now, we have bigger fish to fry. We will need Ben, so we'll extend him a sweet immunity deal."

"Okay," Chuck said. "What's our next move on Tony?"

While maple trees slept, sugar shacks opened up around them and seasonal entrepreneurs attached sap buckets to hollowed elderberry twig hooks beneath the spiles. Waves of gossip and fear spread across the province the old-fashioned way, by word of mouth. Streets grew increasingly empty at night.

Edouard LeBlanc, nicknamed *Sparky*, parked his logging truck on the side of Pine Glen Road. He was a short man with brawny arms and rough hands. Dressed in coveralls, a Husqvarna cap and steel-toe boots, he looked anything but graceful. With lumber sales sluggish due to the American housing economy, his focus was now on harvesting firewood for a living. Power saw, peavey and lunch in hand, he made his way into his leased acreage of crown land.

He looked forward to the end of the school year when his two sons could help him. The beech and maple trees weren't getting lighter, but with his lumberman's stubbornness he continued his daily routine until he had at least three cords cut and moved to the roadside. A good day's work would bring nearly five hundred dollars in the fall when it came time to sell.

When he came out at dusk, his truck was gone. When it was found thirty kilometres farther south the next day, journalists printed the story.

Tony was moving deeper into the region.

On the same day, two hours north of Moncton, Elmer Fitzgerald parked his 1991 maroon Dodge Spirit near a church and followed others inside for Ash Wednesday celebrations. After the ceremony, he walked to the neighbouring cemetery and unlocked the iron gates. Rain dripped off the eaves of the vault, falling onto the grave-digger's green, hand-knitted tuque and trickling down his neck. He pulled his collar up, his watchful eye scanning the area. He'd be digging soon for the two bodies stored in the burial chamber since fall.

Elmer was counting the days to spring when flocks of mourners dropped by, beautifying tombstones with artificial flower saddles. He changed into his rubber boots and walked the perimeter of the ten-acre cemetery, skirting around piles of brown, frosted leaves until he made his way to the vault. He stopped abruptly. The lock was broken. After opening the door, he realized the bodies were gone too. He called 9-1-1 and cops showed up in droves. Word of the missing corpses added to the anxiety none more anxious than the immediate families of the deceased.

People were upset. Ministers and priests were flooded with calls from widowers wanting to see the plots of their departed. Some relatives even went as far as to demand to see security at graveyards. Families wanted to keep their loved ones where they belonged and were ready to press charges if anything happened to them. Cathy's plate was overflowing, to say the least.

"We need to identify the bodies found at Tony's house." Cathy hung up, stared at Larry and raised her voice: "Why has it taken so long?"

"Cathy," Larry said softly. "Take a short break. Go home. Sleep. Do whatever you have to do to unwind. Please, get away from here for a while. It'll clear your mind. You know darn well that they're going as fast as they can, but there's serious work involved."

"I know, Larry," she answered, her face cupped in her hands, elbows on her desk. "But I can't leave. I can only imagine what it would feel like to have my mother's body vanish from a vault. I'd be pissed too."

"Go home, Cathy," Larry continued.

"I won't go home, but I'll go to the gym," she replied.

The day after being released, Ben walked down the shaded trails leading to the back of his woodlot and inhaled the sweet and damp smell of pines. As always this time of year, he laid the chainsaw down and surveyed the stand, spotting several burls to remember to cut later for turning bowls on the lathe. He jumped over decaying logs, checking downed trees and snapping off branches as he went. He was sheltered from the wind whirling up above and he watched as the wind hit the tree canopy and shadows danced on the forest floor. There was more hardwood than usual, and that made him happy. Thinning the forest was all that he needed for firewood. Sure, he'd harvest a few majestic firs to let sunlight reach the bottom floor here and there, but that was it. By taking his time and not clear cutting, he'd have five cords easy by month's end.

The air was perfect with no black flies or mosquitoes yet and the soil hard, ideal to carry him before the spring rains would turn the ground spongy. He inhaled through the nose, letting the smells of freshly cut wood ignite his senses. He felt a momentary release from stress as he sat on a stump, deciding where to cut next. He wanted a joint, but having quick reflexes was more important. Ben lit a cigarette and tightened the laces on his steel-toe boots.

Shortly after, he gripped the handle of the chainsaw and began notching away at a dead beech until it dropped to the ground. The horizontal blade continued along the entire length of the tree, lopping off limbs. He moved the saw to the bottom of the tree and began slicing it down into four feet logs. Under his breath, he thanked Harry Johnson for offering him a job while he was in high school. He had fallen in love with logging.

For weeks on end, Ben kept chopping hardwood logs whenever he had the time and began moving them close to the house. He'd cut them later for firewood.

CHAPTER TWENTY-ONE

O N WEEK TWO OF THE MANHUNT, CHUCK GLANCED at the welcome sign as he approached Riverside-Albert, Population 229 printed in Gothic gold letters on the green sign. He drove from one end of town to the other, glancing at the few short streets along the way. Scruffy homes of the 1920s were wedged between once-proud but now neglected Victorian houses. A convenience store with a gas pump at the bottom of the hill and a bakery were the only businesses open. On top of the hill, a massive Fundy Baptist Church sat perched in all its glory with stain-glass windows reflecting back at the world.

Chuck pulled in next to the church, and read the hanging white frame:

Founded in 1959. Sunday Worship - 10:30am.

He backed up and pulled in the driveway next door. This would be his new home for a while. Reverend Pat King's lodging was more than adequate. Chuck paid for two rooms, one to sleep and watch TV, the other to work. He found a spot for his laptop and wrote emails to Cathy and Larry to report on his whereabouts. At seven o'clock the next morning, he went downstairs for breakfast.

"You have a good appetite, Bob," Heather King said as she sat across from him.

Chuck rubbed his belly. "That's what my wife keeps telling me. But it's not so good for the diet though."

"Did you say your last name was Thomas?" Pat inquired.

"Yeah," Chuck went on. "Bob. I'm a retired biology professor and now doing research with undergraduate students at Fundy Park. I won't be here much."

"Your lunch and supper portions will be neatly tucked away in the fridge for when you do get home," Heather added.

Chuck thanked Heather and grabbed a banana from the fruit bowl as he headed back to his room.

Flurries had begun falling slowly and the sun had just caught the scattered clouds when he decided to walk the half kilometer to the bakery-turned-cafe called The Sticky Monkey. He studied the area on foot – a few older, boarded-up buildings, several fishing boats hiding under plastic tarps in back yards, burlap-covered shrubs, empty flower beds, and, across from the Sticky Monkey Cafe, a former bank, now a museum with a gigantic three-foot grindstone wheel at its doorstep. In behind it, bales of hay in white casings, giving the appearance of huge marshmallows, were sprawled across the hoarfrost-covered field. He grabbed the newspaper, folded neatly on the Cafe's doorstep, and scanned the front page. A cow's bell, hanging above the door, rang as he entered.

"Coffee?" said the heavyset server. He wore a red and black plaid shirt, forest-green Bermuda shorts, along with a beige oversized homespun turtleneck sweater, wool socks, and a pair of black Crocs.

"You bet," Chuck answered, handing the newspaper to him. "It's freezing out there," he continued, rubbing his hands to warm up.

"This paper is for customers," the server noted as he filled a mug in front of Chuck. "Go ahead, read it. What brings you to this neck of the woods so early in the year?"

"Research," Chuck replied. "At Fundy. I'm writing a book. I'm Bob, by the way, Bob Thomas, and I'm staying at the Reverend King's house. Do you own this place?"

"Me name's Harry Dowden and we've been here a little over ten years now, me wife and I," he replied as he returned Chuck's handshake. "Me darlin' Betty loves to bake and I's love people. We figured it'd be a good mix and it's worked out pretty good for us. Winter's slow so we tend to hibernate with the rest of the folks around here, but now, with the manhunt, this place is booming."

"You from the Rock?" Chuck asked with a smile.

"Lard t'underin' Jesus b'y," Harry replied. "I sure ain't from the prairies. I'm all Newfie and I likes to put on the accent for tourists." Harry paused, smiling wide. "I'm from a suburb called Pouch Cove near Sin Jahn's and I came here when I was just a lad looking for work. I fell in love with the mainland cuz you have real nice trees here and you can farm. The wind blows so damn hard dere dat all we got is midget trees. We call them tuckamores. And with nothing but rock and peat bog for land, we have to garden in the ditches."

"So, do you have a Newfenese menu?" Chuck asked, laughing.

"Jiggs dinner," he replied. "Ya know, with chicken, veggies and salt beef all smothered in gravy. I only cook that in the summer, though. Not everybody likes that."

"If I'm still here this summer," Chuck said with a sigh, welcoming the Newfoundland generosity and sense of humour, "I'll give it a try. Did you hear anything new about this Walsh guy?" Chuck found himself asking.

"Well," Harry said, rolling his eyes. "According to the news, he's still on the loose. My wife is worried silly that he'll show up here, but I got me rifle loaded just in case."

Chuck studied the Sticky Monkey Cafe, the sun spilling through its low, front windows and onto the oak floor. Tony could turn up here as much as anywhere. He could easily sleep and eat in the woods for quite a while, but eventually he'd come out somewhere. Chuck thanked God it was still too early in the year for people to hike and camp on the Dobson Trail. The sixty-kilometre trail between Moncton and Fundy National Park would be impossible to patrol.

The cow's bell rang and Chuck, preparing to read the paper, shot a look over the top of his glasses at the newcomer, a young man no heavier than the average ten-year-old with tousled hair damp with snow. He was small, baby-faced, and carried a spiral-bound drawing pad and a charcoal pencil in his bare hands.

"Siddown b'y," Harry said to the youngster as he tapped him on the shoulder. "I'll be right back." Harry went to the kitchen, returning with a hot chocolate. "This should warm you all over. Don'tcha have mittens?"

The male grinned, exposing a set of rotten teeth.

"He's the village idiot," the owner whispered in Chuck's ear as he filled his cup with more coffee. "He can hear but he can't talk. His parents, thank God they're both dead now, made him sleep in the barn and beat the shit out of him if he spoke up. All he ever does is roam around town and draw, but he's got real talent. You should see."

"Where does he live?" Chuck asked quietly.

"With a retired school teacher who keeps buying him all that stuff. He felt sorry for him, I guess. Look, above the coffee pot. That's his doing. It's a jim-dandy, ain't it?"

Chuck walked up to the coffee machine and studied the framed picture of the cafe in charcoal, hanging on the wall.

"One day, I'm going to get myself a website for this little shop and use that as a backdrop for my front page," he added proudly. "This picture would give ol' Vincent Van Cock a run for his money, wouldn't it?"

"I needed that," Chuck said, laughing. "The Dutch painter would turn in his grave if he heard you. This kid sounds more like a genius than an idiot, wouldn't you say?"

Chuck walked by the young lad on the way to his table, noticing a loose, sketchy, scribble of a face on his drawing pad.

"Mind if I join you?" Chuck asked as he pulled a chair at the boy's table.

He didn't get a reply, but he didn't meet resistance either when his eyes gazed into the brown eyes across from him. Chuck tried to make conversation, but was ignored as the lad continued to draw.

"My name's Bob," Chuck said. "Any time I'm here, come on over and sit with me. I just moved here and I'd sure enjoy some company. I'm a marine biologist and I'll be kicking around the park for the next couple of months. Hey, I'm even writing a book about whales. Maybe you could draw me a whale for my book."

Instead of responding, the lad ran out of the cafe and hopped onto a 3-speed bicycle, steering his bike across the road and settling on the steps of the old bank/museum.

Harry walked up to Chuck's table. "He's not gonna talk to you. Like I told you, he's a bit slow, if you know what I mean."

"Yes, you mentioned that... What's his real name?"

"Harold," said the owner. "After his father, but his father was so rotten that after he died, everybody started calling the lad Jesse."

"Jesse?" Chuck found himself muttering. "Jesse what?"

"His last name is mud around here," the owner said, suddenly serious. "It's Rawford, but don't say you heard it from me."

Chuck ambled his way back to his temporary home and, with a click of the mouse, opened his emails. He replied to his wife's numerous messages begging him to keep his promise to stay in touch. She knew he wouldn't keep it, not when he was out of circulation for more than a couple of weeks. But she tried anyway and he liked that.

He read a "high-priority" message from Diane linking Tony with the pre-burial corpses missing in central New Brunswick. According to her note, there was also a possible link between the skeletons found in Tony's house and those taken from a cemetery in the province a couple of years earlier. With another click of the mouse, Chuck found nineteen graveyards in Albert County.

He printed the list. Then, he swallowed lunch, made quick conversation with his new landlord and drove around the area the rest of the day, scouring cemeteries and crossing them off his list.

"I'm in over my head with these cemeteries," he told Cathy.

"What are you doing checking out cemeteries anyway?" Cathy questioned. "That's not your job!"

"I'm just killing time right now," he replied. "Just getting to know the area."

He returned to the warmth of a roast beef dinner and gospel music playing on the old ghetto blaster in the kitchen.

"Who's this kid – Jesse, I guess– that hangs out at the Sticky Monkey Cafe?" Chuck asked.

"Jesse Rawford," Pat replied while looking at his wife. "The poor kid didn't have much of a chance. We pray for him every day, Heather and I, don't we dear?"

Half an hour later, stomach full and the banter having died down, Chuck retired to his room. Leaning against the headboard, he thought about Jesse. He then wrote to Diane to have her check him out and finally drifted off in his cozy quilted bed. By six the next morning, Chuck received a reply from Diane. He had to admit, she was on the ball.

You should stay away from these Rawfords, as their list of criminal activities is a mile long, she wrote. *Two of his uncles are serving life sentences. People think they're crazy from what I read in past officers' reports. This is based on some homicides in the area dating back as far as a century ago. Here's a few attachments on what I could find on his family. Fill your boots.*

Chuck spent the better part of an hour reviewing restricted files on the Rawfords. At a time when capital punishment was in vogue, Jesse's grandfather and great grandfather were hanged in public for killing an entire family of six, apparently with an axe. Jesse, twenty-six, had no record. After breakfast, Chuck returned to the Sticky Monkey.

"Good morning," Chuck said as Harry approached

the table with the coffee pot. "I'll have one of your sticky cinnamon buns, too. Those are to die for."

"I'll pass the compliment to the chef," Harry replied on his way to the kitchen.

Chuck peered over his spectacles again, the black frame sliding slightly down his nose, when he heard the clank of the doorbell. He was nosy, it came with the job. He lowered the newspaper as Jesse made his way to his table. Pleasantly shocked, Chuck watched him as he sat, then picked up the newspaper and pointed at Tony's picture on the front page.

"Yes," Chuck said. "Everybody's looking for him."

Without a moment's hesitation, Jesse flipped through his charcoaled drawing pad and finally stopped, staring at Chuck for a few seconds, before turning the page towards him. Chuck's eyes widened as he looked down at a picture of Tony.

"Jesus," Chuck blurted out. "Did you see him?"

Jesse left as swiftly as he had come in, then bicycled across the road and again sat on the concrete steps of the old museum, drawing. Chuck moved to a table next to the window and pulled his 35mm camera out of its case, attaching the zoom. Through the camera lens, the boy's right hand, red as a lobster, was moving quickly on the paper while his left forearm held on to the pad from underneath. He wore forest-green gym pants with one pocket pulled out underneath a short khaki corduroy jacket. A few buttons were missing, leaving his neck open to the icy wind. His flabby ears and messy black hair, sticking out like thistle weed, stood out from the green, tight knit toque. His runny nose looked big above his weak chin. Chuck lowered the camera, and with laser focus spotted the encryption *Kamik* written on the top side of his unlaced dogsledder-type boots. He adjusted the zoom, focusing on an eyelet missing on the left boot. He took a few shots before putting the camera back in its case.

CHAPTER TWENTY-TWO

THE CLEAR BLUE SKIES WELCOMED BEN AS THE ground slipped away and he flew high above the seagulls, the word *Liberty* proudly displayed on the door of his Chinook. Here, he had to answer to no one. He could pick a direction and then change his mind mid-course. Here, he could do whatever he liked.

After soaring over Fundy Park, he pushed the control stick forward to climb and then sideways to bank the aircraft north towards his favourite spot, Hayward Pinnacle. Climbing to over 1,000 feet, he gazed down at the Petitcodiac River to his right and followed the coast to Riverside-Albert. Then he pointed the nose west and, within minutes, a majestic older forest appeared before him as he neared Prosser Brook Road. Miles of untouched powder blinked at him as he moved over Caledonia Mountain, just below Hayward Pinnacle.

He landed on an open patch near the top of the Pinnacle and stood outside to smoke a reefer, tripping on his newfound freedom. Deep down, though, Ben also knew the baggage his name carried now. He remembered the reporters, their questions and the camera flashes as he walked out of the city lockup.

It was late afternoon when Ben started up *Liberty* and turned north with Moncton in the distance. Once the aircraft's wheels touched ground, he padlocked the hangar and jumped into his Jeep.

Larry, still in his car, was waiting for him at the end of the driveway. Ben strolled to the driver's door, pushing his long hair out of his face.

"G'day, Larry."

"Get in. It's freezing out there."

Ben got in Larry's car, then pointed ahead, "Drive up Scotsburn, Larry. I want to show you something."

When they reached the top of the hill, Ben unlocked the iron gates and led Larry to the storage barn. He opened the doors, and a sense of pride that he hadn't felt in ages suddenly washed over him.

"You fly this thing?" Larry asked, surprised. "For real, in this weather?"

"Yeah," replied Ben, "doesn't bother me any. There's a little heater in the cockpit."

"You own the building?"

"I wish. I lease it."

"Well, I'm a bit speechless," Larry said, obviously seeing Ben in a new light. "Where do you go?"

"All over Albert County mainly," Ben said with a smile. "It's gorgeous from up there."

"I'm impressed, Ben." Larry admired the aircraft for a moment, then said, "Mind if I ask you a few more questions about Tony?"

Ben put his hands in his coat pockets and smiled at Larry. "Before we do that, I've been meaning to call ya... to thank you for getting me out. Thank you from the bottom of my heart. Now, let's go back home. I'm getting hungry."

While frozen pizza cooked in the oven, Larry poked for answers.

"He didn't come around here?"

"He'd be crazy to... don't you think? If he's reading the papers, he knows better than that."

"Any idea where he'd be hiding?"

"Knowing Tony, he could be anywhere."

"Any special place he liked when you were kids?"

Ben thought a moment, then nodded. "Sawmill Creek. There wasn't much there when we were kids, but we used to go there a lot. Usually to swim. There's falls nearby. We'd jump off a cliff into the swimming hole."

Larry drove back to his hotel and found Sawmill Creek on the map, then paged Chuck. When Chuck called, Larry asked if he'd made any progress.

"Not really," Chuck replied. "But I did meet a young guy named Jesse and I have a hunch that he may know something about Tony."

"He told you that?" Larry asked.

"No," Chuck said. "He can't talk. Or doesn't talk. I know, it sounds funny, but this kid, he's a whiz at drawing and he showed me a sketch of Tony this morning."

Larry though it over for a moment. "He's probably seen Tony's picture on the news, don't you think?"

"Thing is," Chuck continued, "he drew Tony with long blond hair and a baseball cap in front of a cabin."

"Blond hair?" Larry cried. "The guy had no hair when we last saw him."

"I know," Chuck said. "I know. There's something about that kid. And get this, there was a RE/MAX sign on the bottom right hand corner."

"The real estate company?" Larry answered.

"I know... right?" Chuck said. "He might be hiding in a vacant house."

"Which one?" Chuck laughed wholeheartedly. "How the heck would I know, Larry? I'm no psychic."

"You know something, my friend?" Larry said without waiting for a reply. "Ben told me of a place where he and Tony used to go when they were kids. An old cabin at Sawmill Creek. I could meet you there first thing tomorrow morning."

"Worth a shot," Chuck said.

"Meet me at the Dobson Trail entrance on Pine Glen Road," he continued. "You know where that is, right?"

"Hello," Chuck replied. "I'm from here!"

Larry chuckled. "Okay then. In the meantime, I'll go to a RE/MAX office and get the property listings. There can't be a ton of them for sale in that neck of the woods."

The next morning, Chuck was right on time and joined Larry for the trip to Sawmill Creek Road. After driving for a few kilometres, Larry turned left on a dirt road and drove for at least five kilometres, gravel ticking up the undercarriage of the vehicle, before coming to a stop. They then walked a short distance until a narrow path appeared on the left.

"Sawmill Creek is about a kilometre from here," Larry said while gazing at his GPS. "Are you up for a walk?"

"I need all the exercise I can get," Chuck replied. "Cathy's aunt is a hell of a cook and I'm addicted to sticky buns at the Sticky Monkey Cafe."

"No hints that anyone walked this path lately," Chuck said as he watched Larry navigate their way to the cabin with the GPS. The trail was a carpet of decomposing black leaves bordered by overgrown bushes. "But you wouldn't see anything even if you wanted to Larry, the way you're pinned to that rig."

"I love these instruments," Larry said without taking his eyes off of it. "I learned to use them when I worked with Search and Rescue a few years back and I got hooked."

"Well then, use it to tell me how far we have to go," Chuck said, almost out of breath.

Larry grinned widely. "We're only a few hundred meters away now."

Within a few minutes, the pair studied an old, run-down cabin and walked around the lot of oversized trees. Two of the three windows were broken and the plywood door, once white and red, was open. They walked around the cabin, scanning the ground. Chuck shook his head. "The only prints I see are animal prints. I think we'll have better luck with the RE/MAX properties."

"Let's hope your hunch is right," Larry said as they walked back to the vehicle. "I won't get the property listing until later this afternoon. Let's meet again in the morning."

"Meet me in Riverside-Albert at the Sticky Monkey Cafe at seven-thirty," Chuck replied. "And call me Bob, remember?"

Chuck waved to Larry as he entered the Sticky Monkey. "Hey. Just in time for a fresh pot of coffee."

"Bob," Larry said as he sat across Chuck, sliding a file to Chuck. "The RE/MAX properties we talked about. All seven of them... it shouldn't take too long to find."

Larry pulled the GPS out of his jacket pocket. "The addresses are programmed into this baby right here."

"Good job, Mr. White," Chuck said as he flipped through the pictures.

Harry appeared at Chuck's elbow with a ceramic coffeepot and filled his cup. "Are you looking for property around here, Bob?"

"Maybe," Chuck replied. "Harry, meet my friend Larry. Larry, meet Harry Dowden, co-owner of this fantastic little cafe and the best cinnamon buns on the planet."

Larry extended his hand. "Pleased to meet you, Harry."

"The pleasure is all mine. I'll bring you a coffee and one of our famous cinnamon buns."

Chuck handed one of the real estate photos back to Larry. "It's pretty damn near the same as what Jesse drew. Where's that on your GPS?"

Larry said as he punched buttons, waited. "From here... It's exactly seven kilometres the way the crow flies."

Chuck rolled his eyes. "Who gives a shit about the crows... Give me the kilometres by car."

Larry laughed. "It's about twelve kilometres, Bob."

As they headed outside, Jesse, on his bicycle, flew by.

"Hey Jesse!" Chuck yelled. But Jesse never turned

back, kept kicking away at his pedals down the main road towards Fundy Park.

"Jesse Rawford?" Larry asked as he climbed into Chuck's new Explorer.

Chuck took a noisy slurp from his takeout coffee. "The one and only."

Searching for and finding RE/MAX properties in remote corners of Albert County, where some secondary roads were barely paths, took the entire morning. But their efforts to find Tony were futile.

"I feel betrayed, Larry," Chuck said.

"Yeah, I think Jesse sent you on a wild goose chase."

CHAPTER TWENTY-THREE

I N WEEK FOUR OF THE MANHUNT, THE WEATHER BROKE in April and the mercury climbed above freezing with single digits. The first breeze of warm, moist air over the Bay of Fundy knocked at the windows, trying to seep indoors.

Ben stared out the window dreamily for a long time, tapping his fingers on the sill. He flexed his elbows and pressed his forearms against the cold windowpane. He observed a housefly meandering upside down on the glass outside. After staring at it for a while, he shook his head and then flipped his hands around and stared at his nicotine fingers. Since the incident, stress had doubled up his cigarette consumption, a habit he'd have to break once this was over.

Unable to adjust to the quietness in the house, he walked out, shoulders slouched, and opened the barn door in the hopes of driving out the last winter's staleness. Sitting on an old stump, he stared at the wilderness around him, his muddy driveway, the winter-damaged beech under the canopy of sugar maples and light spring growth scattered amongst darker evergreens. The wind blew his long hair every which way and he was jealous of the big white clouds above. He inhaled the sharp fragrance of woodland and let out a long sigh, raising his coffee mug to his lips. It was empty. He checked his watch, realizing that for the past twenty minutes he had had no conscious thought other than of Tony.

Newspapers described his brother as the most horrific human predator that ever lived. One of the local newspapers even nicknamed him the *Graveyard Freak*. As cops began to flood Albert County, Ben was ordered not to fly anymore, so he spent most days in the shop or in front of the television, which sometimes was not even on. And he knew they were keeping an eye out for him and had even tapped his phone. Just as bad as being under house arrest with an ankle monitor, he thought.

Around 8 p.m. on April Fool's Day, there was a knock at the door that brought him out of the bathroom a bit spooked. He hated drop-ins without warning. He scanned the house on the way to the door and switched the outdoor light on, his heart pumping all the while.

"Oh," Ben said amicably to his tenant. "Ken. Come on in."

Ken stepped inside. "How are you keeping these days?"

"Can't complain."

"Any news on Tony?"

"Haven't heard a thing."

Ken handed a package, wrapped in a kitchen towel, to Ben. "The wife made it... maple sugar pie. Thought you might need a bit of comfort these days."

Ben took the pie and set it on the table, humbled by the gesture.

"You didn't have to do that."

"We want you to come over tomorrow night and have supper with us."

"Really?" Ben found himself asking.

Ken opened the door and stepped outside. "Is that a yes?"

"Sure," Ben nodded in assent. "What time?"

"Five okay with you?"

"Sure," Ben replied as he walked outdoors with his neighbour, waving him goodbye.

"Ken," Ben shouted. "Thanks. Thanks so much."

After devouring several pieces of the sweet pie, Ben put on his headphones and listened to songs that brought him closer to Maryel – *Say that you love me* by Fleetwood

Mac, then *Time in a bottle* by Jim Croce. He fell asleep on the couch, eyes wet, and woke early, looking forward to the social gathering later in the day.

By early afternoon, he was restless as he shoved a new pack of du Maurier King in his shirt pocket. He left the house and walked up the hill on Scotsburn Road. He raised the hangar's overhead doors, then began to unwrap the cellophane from the cigarette pack and stood looking inside, struck by a memory. When his mother was sick, he'd brought her here to show her his prized possession. He had just bought it. Didn't even know how to fly it yet. He walked up to the spot where she had stood. "You might die before me after all," she had said, her hoarse and deep voice sounding more like a robot as she spoke through her mechanical machine. Tears ran down his cheeks.

On his way to Ken's house, he noticed that the door to the horse-barn was open. Jesus Christ, Tony. Are you doing this? He walked slowly and lit a reefer before walking in. The joint glowed as he took a long drag, letting the smoke slide all the way to his lungs before releasing it. Why are you doing this, Tony? On his way out, he flicked the roach in the remnants of snow and shoved an old wood plank against the door.

When he reached the Lewis' home, he knocked on the screen door, but nobody answered. The front door was open and he pushed it all the way, peeking inside.

"Hello. Ken?"

The house fell silent. He scanned the kitchen and froze, staring at the sight of Ken and his wife, at the table, tied, throats slashed. He launched full speed home and dialled 9-1-1 before returning to the Lewis' home. He waited outside and breathed a sigh of relief when, within fifteen minutes, Larry and Diane showed up with several police cruisers and ambulances.

"I could smell him today, Larry," Ben said. "He's worse than I thought. Why would he do such a thing in Mom's house? What's he trying to prove?"

"I'm sorry, Ben."

Diane, acting as team leader, roped off the crime scene all the way to the wooded area surrounding the property, including the driveway and left an entrance/exit lane leading to the house's front door. One police officer stood at the entrance and began recording the names of everyone passing by. Might need this info to rule out any suspects later in court, Diane had told him. In the yard, a forensic photographer alternated between snapping pictures of the property and using his video camera, zooming in and out of areas of interest while two police officers searched the yard for any evidence.

Meanwhile, forensic investigators, wearing hooded crime-scene suits, boots, latex gloves and masks, waited patiently for pathologist Gail Patrick to arrive and pronounce Ken and his wife dead before barging into the home. Larry stood by Ben and neither one said a word until Gail arrived.

Larry joined the forensic team inside and watched as they began collecting evidence – dusting for prints, checking for any foot prints, collecting DNA. When Larry came out ten minutes later, Ben was still standing in the same spot, at the edge of the road in front of the house.

"Ben," Larry said, "why don't you take a hotel room like you did last time? And call me when you've settled in."

Ben turned and started walking away. "I don't need a sitter. Tony wouldn't hurt me." Ben knew that it wasn't true, but he couldn't show anyone his fear.

Larry slowed, didn't follow. "You sure about that?" he called, but Ben didn't look back.

In week five of the manhunt, Chuck was standing at the front of the boardroom when the room began to fill up. Quickly it was standing-room only.

"We checked every cemetery and real estate property for sale by RE/MAX in Albert County," Chuck announced.

"But we came up empty. We are now having all the other real estate properties checked, not just RE/MAX, as I speak."

"He's a decorated soldier," a cop standing in the back shouted. "He's trained to hide."

Chuck nodded. "Yes, we can all agree to that."

Cathy, comfortably folded in one of the conference room leather chairs, announced that the military was sending backup to join in the search.

"Locals volunteered their four-wheelers and it's a heck of a lot easier to get around in them. Two K-9s have been brought in and are at the crime scene. Plus, we're setting up a command post in Riverside-Albert for the four-wheelers. Make sure civilians are not part of the search. This must be spelled out to them. Is that clear?"

On April 10, Jesse's caretaker, the old school teacher, died and the next day Jesse moved in with Harry Dowden and his wife, in a back room of the restaurant. Chuck was at the cafe at 7:30 a.m. every day unless he was secretly running back to his office to sign papers. Sarah, Paula and Matt had showed real initiative in running his business on their own but it didn't take long until Matt wanted to be part of the biggest manhunt in New Brunswick. Chuck had brought him in as a biology student a few days earlier.

"Keep a pulse on everything when I'm not around. Blend in, talk to locals, see what they know."

On April 12, Chuck sat across from Jesse, who tore a page out of his drawing pad and handed another drawing of Tony, this time standing beside a waterfall. Chuck stared at Jesse for a half a minute while Harry poured his coffee.

"Shepody Road?" Harry asked looking at Jesse. Jesse nodded. "That's Laverty Falls. In Fundy Park."

"Jesse," Chuck pleaded. "Did you really see him there?"

Jesse grew fidgety and got up and went outside. He stood next to the Explorer with his bicycle, rocking back and forth on his heels. Chuck looked up at the cops walking in and glanced at Harry, a question mark all over his face.

"Who knows, Bob," Harry said, shrugging behind the counter. "He wants to go for a drive. He's harmless really. You better hurry up or he's gonna freeze his butt out there. There's a nasty wind coming off the bay. Better put a move on, big fellor."

Chuck started the ignition from inside the cafe and walked out to meet Jesse. He slapped his hand on the side of the Explorer. "Brand new," he said, "thanks to insurance. Kinda wrecked my last one."

Chuck winked, but Jesse only fidgeted.

"Do you want to show me where this guy is?" Chuck asked while he unlocked his door. "Is that what you're so urgent to tell me?"

Now standing to the back of the vehicle, Jesse pointed to his bike.

Chuck nodded. "Sure, why not. But just wait a minute, I'll be right back."

Before leaving, Chuck walked into the cafe and told Matt to follow them.

Along the way, Chuck tried to make mental notes of the landmarks as he interpreted Jesse's hand instructions. A small gravel road came into view as they crossed an isolated steel bridge. Chuck turned sharply and gravel crunched beneath the tires. He slowed down, following the narrow, dusty road and watched with hesitation as the bridge slipped away from his rearview mirror. Jesse signalled him to stop and he coasted on the edge of the dirt road and killed the engine. A railroad trestle could be seen in the distance and a narrow, twisted pathway appeared to his right.

"Is he in there?" Chuck said pointing to the footpath. Jesse nodded like a bobble-head doll.

Chuck slipped his leather gloves on. "It's cold out here, Jesse. You stay in the truck, understand?"

Once outside, Chuck pulled his parka's hood over his head. He waved at Jesse with one hand and locked the vehicle doors with the other hand, then took a trail through black spruce and balsam fir trees, the path narrowing the deeper he went. He twisted his head around for any activity. While on the footpath and away from Jesse's sight, he called Matt.

Chuck stopped, listened. "Where you at?"

"I can see your truck," Matt replied.

"Good. I'm going to keep on walking. Catch up with me. Jesse stayed in the truck. Don't let him see you."

"You're heading to Square..." Matt continued but Chuck hung up.

Chuck approached the falls and ducked to get behind a large granite rock. Quiet as a decaying stump, he listened and watched for movement. Fifteen minutes later, he stood to get rid of a leg cramp. He inched his body up and stretched the cramped muscle, rubbing it until the pain subsided.

He moved around the granite rock and gazed out at the large pine trees whose exposed roots sat around in the dirt. He leaped from his hiding place and scrambled up the slightly curved pathway until he reached the top of the cliff next to the waterfall. There, he stared down at the hill and looked around. He caught the glimpse of a flash, thinking it was a cigarette lighter.

"BOB!" a male voice shouted to his right.

Birds fled in panic. As he turned, he realized Jesse had done the talking. Almost immediately, Chuck heard the crack of the shot and the fluttering whir of a round whizzing past his left ear like an angry bee, sending bark flying several yards away.

"Jesse! Get down!"

Chuck hit the dirt, crawling until he reached a large tree. He kneeled, pulled his gun from his shoulder strap and scanned the area. There was movement in shrubs nearby, and his heart skipped a beat, but he quickly realized it was Jesse. Chuck tried to catch his breath. He sat with his back against a large fir tree, then dialled Matt again. There was no answer and for long minutes Chuck didn't move. In front of him, a skunk, waking from a deep sleep, performed a comical winter push-up routine to speed up its blood circulation. Suddenly, sirens rang out and shortly after a policeman's voice echoed below the falls.

"You are surrounded!" the voice shouted over the loudspeaker. "Drop your weapons and come out with your hands behind your head. It's time to give yourself up, Tony!"

Chuck sat still and took in his breath sharply, holding it in and waiting for a response. His phone rang.

"Matt."

"You okay?"

"I... uh... I'm safe. Just hiding behind a tree."

"I called for backup when you told me to tail you."

Chuck hung up as uniformed officers and military soldiers, dressed in tactical gear and armed with high-powered rifles, came through the trees. One member of the army tactical team hurried to him and told him to stay put. The noise of a helicopter whirring overhead grew louder.

"You're surrounded!" the officer repeated on the speaker. "If you resist, you do not stand a chance of making it out of here alive!"

Police officers and military personnel grew by numbers and, while some fanned out, most marched side by side to the waterfall. As they circled the falls, Chuck considered moving from behind the tree just enough to follow the action, but the same crew member who had moments earlier motioned him to stay put had eyes on him. The hairs on the back of Chuck's neck stood up.

Ten minutes passed with more shouting. Chuck stared down at the leaf-mat beneath his feet, and without moving his head, he looked up at the patches of snow amongst the moss-covered and decaying tree trunks and broken branches. He shivered. He certainly couldn't live long in a place like this.

Then the troops retracted and the soldier joined him, waving him to wait while he adjusted the rubber earpiece loop around his ear. Chuck's eyes grew wider and with a crack in his voice said, "And? Did we get him?"

"Unfortunately not."

Chuck emerged from the woods and joined the flow of officers back to his vehicle where Larry, Matt and Jesse were now waiting. He nodded to Jesse and pressed his hands together, palms touching and fingers pointing upwards, thumbs close to the chest. "Namaste! You saved my life. And, Larry, you missed all the fun!"

Chuck checked his watch. Almost two hours had passed since he'd left the cafe. He looked around; it seemed so peaceful. Where was Tony? Damn bastard got away. "Guys, I'm going to drive my hero home and then get myself a stiff drink. Jesse? Cripes, where did Jesse go?"

Chuck looked in the back of his vehicle and the bike was gone. "He warned me, you know. Called out before the shot was fired. He saves my life and then takes off on his bike."

Larry leaned back on Chuck's Ford Explorer. "Not to be a killjoy, but Cathy is waiting for us in her office." He put his hand on Chuck's shoulder. "Jump in with me. One of the cops will drive your vehicle back."

"And blow my cover? I'll meet you there in an hour. Like I said. Need a drink."

Chuck peeled away, throwing gravel and dust in his wake as he left the site. He vowed to get rid of the fear in the pit of his stomach. His left eye twitched uncontrollably and he tried to concentrate, tried to imagine what Tony was up to and deeply felt how lucky he was to be alive.

CHAPTER TWENTY-FOUR

A T 3 P.M. ON APRIL 12, LARRY, DIANE, CHUCK, AND Don had gathered in Cathy's office to brainstorm. It was a corner office on the ninth floor with a view of downtown Moncton and full of new furniture: a large mahogany desk with a matching storage credenza, a two-seat upholstered light grey couch with two chairs and a table long enough to sit eight people.

"Though we were unable to catch him," Cathy said with a hint of optimism, "we found fingerprints on items in a few hunting cabins, and we're doing the same with the properties for sale in the area."

Larry nodded. "Makes sense he'd be hiding in the camps. Half of the time no one's there." Larry then flipped up his hand before anyone else spoke. "The camps' owners told us that two guns and some ammunition were missing. Both camps' wood stoves had been recently used. One guy had a cord of wood and it's gone. The other had over two cords and that's gone too. They also reported finding a few empty whiskey and beer bottles."

"Unbelievable," Diane noted. 'He's been living in the wilderness for a month *and* he's been warm and drunk half the time."

"He knows what he's doing," Cathy said, shaking her head. "That's clear. Larry, did you talk to Ben today?"

Larry crossed his hands behind his neck and reclined his chair. "I called him this morning. No answer."

"Try again," Cathy said. "And make sure we still have

eyes on him."

Larry stood and moved towards the door. "Can Diane take care of that? I'd like to move to the conference room and check out the rest of Ben's videos."

"Sounds good," Cathy said. "Keep me posted. Chuck, glad you're safe. Please don't take any unnecessary risks but keep up the good work with Jesse. Now, all of you *scram*."

"Yes ma'am," Chuck replied on his way out.

In the conference room, Larry picked one of a half dozen VHS tapes and inserted it in the VCR. He pushed play and sat deep into his seat. Within seconds, he was sitting up straight.

At the same moment, Chuck leaned in the doorway. "Anything good, Larry?"

"Get the crew in here," Larry said without looking at him. When Diane, Don, and Cathy arrived, Larry told Chuck to kill the lights. Larry pulled his chair closer to the monitor. "You guys ready?"

"We certainly are," Chuck said as he let himself sink into one of the large chairs. His jaw dropped when he saw Jesse and a girl making out.

"What?" Cathy asked, elbowing Chuck.

Chuck slapped his hands on the table. "Where did you get this tape, Larry?"

"At Ben's. I found a box of these hidden in the attic, under insulation, the day we searched his house."

"For those who don't know, that's Jesse," said Chuck. "Where is this taken?"

"Rawford?" Diane asked.

"Yes," Chuck replied as the video continued rolling. "That's him again with another girl. So, it really happened. Goddamn it... Jesse knows Ben, too? Oh, this is weird."

Don moved his hands together in the form of a steeple. "Who's this Jesse?"

"It's a long story." Chuck turned on the camera he had around his neck. He passed the camera around the table showing pictures of Jesse in Riverside-Albert.

Don moved in closer and scratched his temple, "Great close-up. Oh," Don paused, "note this...his left boot has a missing eyelet."

"How's that?" Chuck grunted.

"Well, we found an eyelet in Jack's house the night he was murdered."

Chuck stood up and paced. "Did you find any loose coat buttons at the Thibodeau's?"

"Not that I'm aware of but that doesn't mean there weren't any. It could have been discarded as being one of theirs."

Chuck stopped pacing. "Jesse's coat has a few buttons missing and yes an eyelet on one of his boots. I took close-up pictures of him when I first met Jesse."

"Okay," Don said. "I'll look into the inventory. Otherwise, we'll have to go back to the house."

"The last I heard," Diane said, "Jack's parents had the house up for sale."

Cathy told Larry to stop the tape, then stood and turned on the light. "Don, take Chuck's camera right now and check the inventory. This is a priority." When Don nodded and left the room, camera in hand, Cathy continued.

"Let's bring Jesse in. And Chuck, you're not picking him up. I already have a crew down there. Let's keep your cover in case we can't charge him."

Chuck looked up at Larry. "We can check on Ben and ask him about Jesse."

"Yes," Cathy said. "But tread lightly."

Cathy stood and rubbed the back of her neck. "Diane, get a hold of the officer assigned to watch Ben and report back to me asap."

It was 5 p.m. when Chuck and Larry walked outdoors, glad to be out of the office. They climbed into Chuck's Explorer and Chuck rolled down the window. The cool air filled the cabin as he took to Route 114. Chuck absentmindedly scanned the roadside trees as they flickered by.

Larry pulled a stick of gum out of his coat pocket and offered one to Chuck, but Chuck shook his head. "Damn, where is Tony?"

Behind them there was a sudden blast of a siren and, within seconds, a police cruiser appeared in Chuck's rearview mirror. Chuck pulled his vehicle over to the soft shoulder and made a complete stop. The cruiser weaved in front of him and punched the gas pedal.

At Ben's, while Larry knocked several times, Chuck stretched his neck and looked up. He heard the high, thin whistle of cedar waxwings and let out a sigh of relief. Larry knocked again and looked at Chuck with a shrug. "Maybe he's out running errands or something."

Chuck nodded. "Might be tending to his plane."

They drove up Scotsburn Road and Larry peeked inside the building where Ben kept his plane.

"It's in there," Larry said as he got back in the car.

"Do you still have his house key? He gave you the key when he was interviewed, didn't he?"

Larry smiled. "No way, Chuck. I'm not trespassing. You do it on your own time."

"He's not at his house," Larry told Cathy on the phone. "But his little plane is where it belongs. Should we wait for him?"

"No," Cathy said. "I want you guys to head back here."

Larry and Chuck returned to Moncton and stopped at the hotel where Ben had stayed before going to the cop's station. There was no sign of him there and, by 7 p.m., they were back in Cathy's office with Diane.

"We can't locate Jesse Rawford," Cathy told them. "We talked to the owner of the cafe where he lives now, who told us that Jesse's like a stray cat and he has no idea when he'll be back. But let's move to the conference room again and review what we have so far."

Diane put up a hand. "I've been digging deeper into Ben and Tony and found out that their mother Rose Walsh's maiden name was Rawford. So I took the liberty of asking your uncle, the minister, to check his church records for any of her relatives living in the area. Phyllis Rawford, Jesse's mother, and Rose Rawford... were sisters."

"Jesse, Ben and Tony are first cousins..." Chuck muttered.

"Exactly," Diane replied before resuming her account. "According to his hospital records, Jesse suffers from dissociative amnesia. He's been institutionalized several times since childhood."

"Oh, that's great," Larry said. "He'll plead insanity."

"He won't plead anything," Chuck added. "He doesn't talk."

Larry raised his eyebrows and stared at Chuck. "I thought he saved your life when he called your name?"

"Can I see that file, Diane?" Chuck asked as he reached over the table. "What the heck is this amnesia anyway?"

Diane continued as if she'd practiced what she was about to say for days. "According to his medical reports, he talked at the hospital. It's on record. I think he refuses to talk. He's got a grade six education, so he should be able to read and write to some degree. Also, he's tried many times to commit suicide by slashing his wrist. He never succeeded because he wanted to be found and did it to get attention and sympathy. Still according to medical records, he has a deep sense of abandonment and anybody that shows him affection in any way becomes his friend really quick. He's on anti-psychotics – or is supposed to be – and sometimes these have their share of side effects."

Cathy rubbed her hands together and nodded for

Diane to continue.

"As for the amnesia, it's also known as psychogenic amnesia and the definition is an inability to retrieve stored memories and events, but not due to any physical issues like brain injuries."

"Wow," Chuck said, and then was quiet for a moment, lost in thought. "Let's not jump to conclusions. And, bringing him here is not going to help, trust me. But I'm close to him. Let me talk to him. Let me think about it. In the meantime, I'm starving and I want to call Sharon."

An hour later, Chuck followed the aroma of food to the conference room and made a dive for the Kentucky Fried Chicken on the table.

"Bob," Cathy said while wiping her hands with a napkin. "I can't wait to hear what you have to say."

Chuck loaded his plate with chicken. "First," he said, pointing a drumstick, "let's not barge in on Jesse."

Cathy nodded. "Okay. We'll call off picking him up at the cafe."

"I'll get a kid's book on whales." Chuck nodded, taking his first bite. "I already told Jesse that I was a biologist writing a book about whales. I'll go back to the Dowden's and stay put for a while until he comes around. I'll also try to get one of his boots... not sure how yet... but I'll leave it in a box at the King's house for one of you to pick up. Unmarked cars please! This kid, and your uncle for that matter, cannot have any doubts about who I am."

"I like it so far," Cathy said.

"I need at least a couple of days to set a trap," Chuck continued. "And I need a cop, undercover. Is Diane available?"

Cathy paused for a moment and looked at Chuck. "You got it. Anything else?"

"Since you asked, I also want a boat. Get in touch with Randy Reardon. His son is a Fisheries Officer in Alma and

I'm a whale expert. Tell him to get me a boat and to leave it at the Alma wharf."

On April 16, behind the Old Bank of NB at the junction of routes 114 and 915 in Riverside-Albert, the clouds parted and the light of the full moon spread its glow onto Crooked Creek. And although it wasn't bright enough to see eel or trout swimming in the creek, one could see the arching branches and lance-shaped leaves of old black willows flowing in it. Jesse pedalled his bike, standing up to go faster, and when he reached the first bend in the moonlit creek he jumped off and ran to an eroding pier, his backpack bobbing from one shoulder.

At that very moment, Jesse turned towards the thrumming sound of a helicopter miles away and Tony sprung up from the creek, pulling Jesse into the water like a crocodile on his prey. Jesse smiled. "T-T-Tony!"

"Don't Tony me and keep your voice down."

"Yo-yo-you hungry? G-g-got ya b-b-banana and m-m-muffins li-li-like you asked."

Tony grabbed Jesse's shirt and dragged him, knee-deep in the cold dark water, under a large fleshy hawthorn bush, its long, sturdy thorns poking Jesse's back. In a hurried tone, Tony said, "What are you doing hanging around cops, huh? I heard you call one by his name, 'Bob', the other day. What did you tell them about me, huh?"

Thorns poking his back, Jesse screeched while he tried to twist away. "N-n-nothing T-T-Tony. I sw-sw-swear."

The sound of the helicopter grew louder and, within minutes, its belly hovered over their hiding place, its beams searching. For a few moments Crooked Creek turned to day. Tony put a hand around Jesse's neck and squeezed. "Don't you dare move."

Jesse whimpered as the helicopter disappeared into the night. Tony said, "Didn't say anything, huh? Then how did 'Bob' know to look for me there?"

"L-l-l-let me go!" Jesse begged. "Y-yo-you're hur-hurting me."

Tony climbed back up the slick, muddy bank, tugging Jesse behind him. Once up, Tony threw Jesse down hard, straddled Jesse's ribcage and began slamming his fist into Jesse's face and jaw.

Blood pooled in Jesse's mouth. "S-s-stop, T-T-Tony," Jesse gasped, fighting to keep his arms in front of his face.

"You just don't get it, Jesse. I told you to keep your mouth shut, but you can't do that, can you? Well let me shut it for you."

CHAPTER TWENTY-FIVE

WATER AND DAMPNESS EVERYWHERE.

As if winter hadn't been bad enough, Mother Nature plagued Albert County with north winds and rain, turning the skies a dark grey. The lack of sunlight choked the growth of spring-blooming perennials and people were fed up to the back teeth.

At 5:20 a.m., April 17, Cathy ran her index finger down her office window, following a rain droplet. She couldn't sleep. She'd been to the gym in the middle of the night, showered and finished reviewing the new game plan.

The better part of six weeks had passed since Tony's disappearance. Every time the phone rang, or someone called her name, she closed her eyes, hoping that he was caught. Where the hell was he? What was he doing at this very minute? When would he strike again? Had he had enough or was he laughing at them?

She paced her office and wanted to scream or hit something, but instead she took long breaths and exhaled slowly to calm her nerves. She walked up to the conference room's whiteboard cabinet and opened it. Using a black marker, she wrote – Re-visit Vacant Real Estate, Hunter's Camps/Cottages, Tap Ben's Phone, Keep Watch Ben's House, Tenant's House, Increase Frequency Command Post reports, Increase # Police Cruisers with help from NS/PEI and Add Night Vision Gear for Staff. She inhaled the marker's paint thinner and diesel fuel scent and leaned against the conference room table to look at the board. She heard a sharp knock at the door.

She raised her voice. "Who is it?"

"Larry."

She opened the door just a crack. "What is it? I'm busy."

Larry appeared behind the door holding two coffees. "Too busy to accept my invitation for dinner tonight?"

She took a coffee from him and thought for a split of a second before turning her back to him. "Thanks. Yes. No. Another day, maybe. I have a meeting with the commissioner in ten."

"Later then," he said, closing the door behind him.

Cathy was sweating as she re-entered her office and walked to the window. Black clouds smeared every inch of the sky, making the night darker than it already was. Within minutes, the sky opened up, letting out sheets of rain. She backed away as it hit the windows. On the first ring she picked the phone from its cradle.

"Cathy," he greeted flatly.

"Commissioner."

"Listen, Cathy. I have politicians all the way to the Prime Minister breathing down my neck. A hundred soldiers arrived in Gagetown last night and are heading to Riverside-Albert today. They'll be briefed by Major Peter Van Wart, so I strongly suggest that you touch base with the major as soon as we hang up. You have a week to squeeze Tony Walsh out of the woods or I'll be taking over. Do I make myself clear?"

She sat with her back straight and rubbed her sweaty hand on her skirt. "Absolutely, Commissioner. Loud and clear."

He hung up before she had a chance to say another word. It felt as if a fist were twisting around in her stomach. She picked up the phone and called Diane.

"Emergency meeting! I want everyone involved in this case in the conference room by 8:00 a.m. and that includes Chuck and Patterson from the command post. They can call in."

Cathy felt her heart thumping behind her chest. She picked up the phone and dialed Major Van Wart. After the usual hellos, the major jumped right into it. "I've been waiting for your call."

"I hear troops are on the way and that we have till Monday to find him."

"Puts a whole new spin on things, doesn't it?" The major paused, and when Cathy didn't respond, he continued. "Well, given the short timeline and the increase in manpower, I've received approval to divide the county in six areas and begin searching from the outside in. This tactic should push him out to get some air. I won't touch towns and villages, though. They're all yours."

"That's fine. That's the least we can do. I'll have cops knocking on every door in the county."

"And I assure you that every river, creek and brook will be lit every night until we find him."

Cathy walked into the conference room to coughs and murmurs, then silence. She moved to the podium. "Listen up. Orders just came in that we have seven days to find Tony or we're all getting a pink slip." She swung open the whiteboard cabinet and went through each item, delegating as she went.

"The army will scour the county except for town and villages. That's ours. I want every abandoned car, RV, boat or dory sitting in a yard searched and every empty school gone over with a fine-tooth comb. We're not dealing with a ghost here."

For a split of a second, Cathy looked at Larry and their eyes locked. She then looked away. Had Larry, in fact, asked her out? She believed so. She blushed.

On the cusp of dusk that day, the low light spilling through the trees, a male ring-necked pheasant strolled along the edge of the driveway, much less fearful than Ben, who watched it from his deck as it took flight and landed on top of his Jeep and started hammering its hard beak on the roof. Ben swore, picked up a branch snapped months earlier by the ice storm, and ran to the vehicle with it. Even then, the bird didn't budge, but remained stock-still on the roof. Ben swore again, hurried over to the house and grabbed an ice pick leaning against the wall. He came at the bird swinging and gave him a blow as hard as he could on the behind. The pheasant flew and landed in front of the Jeep. Ben then dashed toward it, yelling. Finally, it took flight. As he turned back toward the house, he caught a glimpse of the barn door.

It was wide open.

He rushed inside and packed a bag. On his way out, he paused at the door, took a deep breath and switched on the outdoor light. Hell-bent on talking to Maryel, he sped down Scotsburn Road but two police cars, their LED light bars flashing in darkness, blocked access to Route 114. As soon as the first cop noticed him, he pulled his gun.

"Get out of your car! And keep your hands where I can see them."

Ben stepped out, hands up in the air. The cop told him to stand behind the car.

"Where's your driver's license?" the cop asked.

"In my wallet," Ben replied. "Back pocket."

"Benjamin Walsh," the cop said after a pause of recognition. "You stay right here."

Ben stood next to his vehicle while another cop searched it and wrote down his license plate number. The other cop, license in his hands, returned to his cruiser. Within minutes, he came back out, apologized for the intrusion and let him go.

Ben barrelled down Route 114, trying to calm his nerves, but after only a few minutes a soldier jumped on the road in front of him. Ben jammed on the brakes, the tires screeching. When he came to a complete stop, the stranger jumped in.

"Move it!" Tony yelled as he took off his balaclava.

Ben's face fell and a sense of terror ran through his

body like a lightning rod. "You?" he managed to say.

The grip on the steering wheel tightened and, under a racing heartbeat, Ben stared at Tony blankly, shaking his head in disbelief. Tony avoided eye contact.

"Just shut your mouth and drive," Tony continued without looking at Ben. "Take Niagara."

Niagara Road, a lonely, potholed two-lane with more trees than people, had no painted lines and was treacherous at night. The tires gripped its rough surface and brought with it a loud rolling noise. Ben tried to stay calm.

"Where are we going?"

"How about you'll see where when we get there."

CHAPTER TWENTY-SIX

WHEN THE DOORBELL RANG AT 6:30 P.M., CATHY knew exactly who was at the door. Behind it, Larry produced an expensive bottle of wine. If he was trying to lower her resistance, he didn't have to try so hard.

"Larry," she said with a warm smile. "Come on in." She escorted him to the back of the condo to large windows overlooking the Petitcodiac River. In the next room, her voice blared from the television, "My staff is working around the clock." She turned the volume down.

"Lovely spot you got here," he said. "Nothing, I mean nothing, beats being close to the water like this."

At that same moment, she jumped at the sound of the bell.

Larry turned. "Must be the pizza. Called it in when I left the office. Barbeque chicken on a thin crust and a Greek salad?"

Cathy nodded, then watched him pay the delivery man. What a physique, she thought. And he was standing here, in her condo. She wanted to run over to him and jump in his arms. Easy, she warned herself. She grabbed two plates and placed them on the kitchen island. "Smells absolutely delicious."

"Any updates in the past hour?" he asked.

"No. But Diane should be here soon."

Larry picked up the bottle of wine, gave her questioning look.

"No. Not tonight," she responded "Raincheck?"

"Of course."

Cathy went to the coffeemaker, filled it with water and measured the grounds before flipping it to brew. She sat down again, pensive, and opened the salad container. Stabbing at her salad, she said, "Humour me. Where do you think Ben is?"

Larry shrugged. "I don't know. In a cave, maybe?"

The doorbell rang again. "Probably Diane," she added as she slid off the barstool to answer the door.

"Mmm!" Diane said as she entered. "Didn't mean to interrupt your dinner."

"No worries. I've got coffee brewing and Larry just came in with a pizza. Please, join."

"Thanks," Diane said, shaking her head and handing Cathy a folder. "Just dropping off the paperwork you wanted and just hung up with the command post. They found a flashlight around Crooked Creek with Tony's prints on it."

"That's encouraging," Cathy responded. "Thank you, Diane. You sure you don't want to stay?"

Diane smiled again, her eyes briefly settling on Larry. "I'm sure. Too much running around to do."

Cathy emptied the pizza bones in the garbage can and put the plates in the dishwasher. Larry leaned his upper body on the countertop near her. No point in being shy, she decided. "I really enjoy being around you, Larry," she said as she pushed a hand through her hair, the words hanging between them.

He angled his head and smiled at her. "You know that's music to my ears." He moved in and his mouth embraced hers, firm and strong. Larry held her head in his hands for an instant and stared into her eyes. Her heart melted. Then, he pulled her in, his hands working their way around her body, feeling every curve. She pushed him away ever so slightly but Larry bent his head down and kissed her on the neck. She let out a sigh of anticipation. She wanted him so bad, but not like this, not in the middle of a crisis. A swirl of emotions danced around in her head and she stopped him.

"Raincheck on this one, too?" she asked quietly. "Just too much going on. *But*, don't leave. I want you to stay. I need to brainstorm. You in?"

"Yes, ma'am," Larry said in his usual unhurried voice.

Chuck called his office, staying in touch, making sure there were no hiccups while he was away. Then, he sat in his room at King's property and watched out the window. Leaves on the birch trees were blowing upward again, their underside shuddering. Before long, the sky cracked outside and lightning flashed and then a thunderclap rolled for five or six seconds. More thunderclaps and more lightning until the rain came.

It wasn't until April 18 that a sunny dawn finally broke. Chuck stood on the King's front deck holding a cup of coffee and observed a large flock of young European starlings probing the lawn for worms. He caught a glimpse of the sun through the trees and then, a few yards away, common grackles, atop a pine tree, swooped and dashed at a crow, hoping to drive the predator away from their nest.

Chuck walked quietly to the Sticky Monkey and gazed at the fenced-in Herefords – their dewlaps hanging like sheets on a clothesline – grazing on the grass in the pasture next to the hay fields. He shifted his eyes to an older, skinny woman, her white hair almost translucent, holding a spring-loaded pruner in her gloved-hand as she circled her flower beds like a mad woman. Farther down the road, a man in his seventies tapped the brim of his blue Maple Leafs cap before hammering down a sign on his lawn that read *Quilts for Sale*.

Swallows whizzed by Chuck, their long forked tails manoeuvring them as they glided around the cafe.

Wearing his brand new snapped-up olive Tilley hat, Chuck felt alive, refreshed. The bell over the door rang and

Harry popped his head out from the back, shouting for Chuck to pour his own coffee. Chuck waited for him at the counter while listening to the radio:

Today will be the warmest April 18th on record since 1948. At 6:30 a.m., it's already 12 degrees Celsius with a high reaching 21. New Brunswickers can finally bring their sandals and shorts out as temperatures will be relatively balmy all week.

"It's going to be a hot one," Harry said excitedly as he wiped his hands on a chef's side towel.

Chuck stroked his chin thoughtfully. "Not soon enough. Is Jesse kicking around this morning?"

"No. He's at the wharf in Alma. Just got hired on as a helper. Not sure how long that'll last."

"Any idea when he'll be back?"

"If they drive him home, he'll be back around three. If not, we won't see him till suppertime or later."

Chuck handed Harry a book on whales. "Could you do me a favour? I'd like to give this to Jesse. Figure he could draw me a picture of one someday."

"*B'y o' b'y!*" Harry rejoiced, bowing his head in humbleness. "That's awful nice of you. I'll make sure he gets it."

"By the way," Chuck added. "Jesse had a pair of winter boots that I really liked. Might get some for next year, you know. Any idea where he got those?"

"How would I know?" Harry asked with a shrug. "No idea, but they're probably kicking around the house somewhere. What do they look like?"

"They're about a foot high and made of leather with a thick rubber sole. They lace up. I know they got to be warm."

"You stay put young man and I'll see if I can find them in his room," he replied as he disappeared. Within a few minutes, he returned. "Are them the boots?"

"Yes indeed," Chuck said. "I'll try to remember what they look like when I'm shopping."

"Here, take them with you. Maybe there's a few end-of-winter sales out there. You know he won't be wearing these anytime soon. He took off pedalling in rubber boots this morning."

"You sure? I wouldn't want to offend him."

Harry coughed. "Go on. I know you'll bring them back. Go on. Take them!"

The phone rang as Chuck was climbing into the Explorer. He adjusted his eyeglasses and glanced at the caller id. "How you doing old boy?"

Larry laughed. "Careful. You're older than I am!"

"I'm on my way to Alma," Chuck continued. "I'm doing some snooping on Jesse. He's apparently working at the wharf, but first I'm dropping off his boots at the King's house. Please have them back to me by suppertime."

"Cathy wants to meet with us," Larry said. "But first, we're meeting Patterson at the command post."

"Great, and since you'll be in Riverside-Albert, meet me at the Seawinds for lunch. It's the only restaurant in Fundy Park."

"I'll check with Cathy and get back to you on that," Larry answered.

CHAPTER TWENTY-SEVEN

C HUCK FOLLOWED ROUTE 114 ALONG THE COASTLINE, his window open. He inhaled deeply, reveling in the aroma of seaweed, hay and turned earth. To his left the widening Petitcodiac River flowed into Chignecto Bay, exposing tide-chiselled cliffs, before emptying into the Bay of Fundy. On the right, timberland, standing tall, clothed the rolling hills. All along the road, ponds spread out between valleys of farm land. Along Calhoun Marsh, he slowed as a line of cattle crossed the scarred, torn-up road. A farmer, standing by an open gate, guided the troop to a metal feeder in a mud-laden pasture.

Once in the Village of Alma, he moved beyond Main Street and drove up the hill to Fundy Park. He positioned the vehicle at the park's main entrance, overlooking Alma, a charming fishing village once dedicated to boat building and lumber exports. He brought the binoculars to his eyes, focusing on the harbour. At the wharf, with Owl's Head Bluff as the backdrop, fishing boats rested in cradles upon the bare ocean floor. On the next high tide they'd rise thirty feet to become almost even with the wharf's deck. Chuck scanned slowly, but did not see Jesse.

Chuck set his eyes on a pair of bright red kayaks atop a Jeep and zoomed in. A young couple got out of the vehicle and, holding hands, walked to the liquor store.

He scanned away from the couple and zoomed in on the distant Nova Scotia shoreline. In between sand bars in the Bay of Fundy, Chuck spotted the lighthouse on Grindstone

Island. He refocused the lens and watched a great blue heron, its blue-grey plumage coming alive under the bright sun, land near the shore and stand statue-like until it made its way belly deep into the waters, probing and pecking. Then quickly it snatched a fish – a flounder, Chuck guessed – and swallowed it whole. Chuck watched as the heron took flight, neck tucked in and long legs trailing behind.

Chuck strolled into the Seawinds, content. At the door, the first thing he saw was a forty-gallon fish tank, full of lobster.

"When's lobster season start around here?" Chuck asked as the waiter escorted him to a table next to wall-to-wall windows overlooking the bay.

"Actually, we have two seasons. One runs from mid-April to the end of July, and the other from mid-October to year's end," the waiter responded. "Can I bring you something to drink?"

"A coffee and a bottle of water... I'm waiting for a few friends to show up."

He glanced at the menu and guzzled down the bottled water. The restaurant was not busy this time of day – a few dozen tables and only a handful of patrons. With a coffee cup in hand, he walked leisurely between empty tables with their lunch setup, glancing at the photos on the walls – the harbour at low and high tide, waterfalls and an old copper mine. He hummed along with Steve Azar's "I Don't Have to Be Me ('til Monday)."

Chuck returned to his seat next to a large trio of windows. Ahead, the bay glimmered in the sunlight. Main Street in Alma was quiet. Cottages and homes were huddled together on the hillside overlooking the bay and a score of lobster boats rocked in the harbour.

At a distance, he spotted an eagle and considered going back to the vehicle to get his binoculars. He'd have to bring Sharon here. She'd love it. He'd have to find time to call her tonight and calm her worst fears. He was due for a vacation, damn, maybe even retirement. She was probably right that he'd had enough. But, then, what would he do all day after retirement?

He was still taking in the scenery when Larry and Cathy swung in.

Chuck broke into a big grin. "Glad you could make it, Cathy."

Larry's eyes locked on the view.

"When I was a kid, we used to come down as far as Riverside-Albert," Cathy confided. "My grandparents lived there and had an outhouse with a two-seater and I'd freeze my 'you know what' in the winter."

"On a more serious note," Cathy whispered as they took their seats. "It turns out the fingerprints on the drawing of Tony that Jesse gave you match those found at the camp, the Thibodeau's house and Ben's home."

"And we found one of the missing buttons on Jesse's jacket," Larry added, leaning in. "It was in the Thibodeau's baby crib."

"Well, you guys come bearing good news. Hopefully I get him to talk now."

When the meals arrived, Chuck forked up a huge bite of beer-battered haddock and dipped it in tartar sauce. Mumbling through a mouthful of fish, Chuck said, "So what's the commissioner like?"

Cathy straightened her back and picked up her fork, adopting a neutral expression. "I can't comment on that."

Chuck noticed Larry watching Cathy's every move. Even when Larry took a bite out of his hamburger and chewed slowly, he was watching her. Cathy pushed aside half of the black olives from her Greek salad and sat up straight, setting her hands on her lap.

"As far as the boat goes, Chuck, one's on the way and will be docked at the wharf later tonight just like you asked. Another boat, compliments of Fisheries and Oceans, will follow you at a distance. The boat is equipped with an Emergency Position Indicator Radio Beacon. We'll know where you are."

"And who's the captain of that boat?" Chuck asked.

"Wilbur Mitcham," Cathy replied. "He just returned from a sick leave and I'm putting him in charge of the operation. Diane will join him and tape your conversations with Jesse. And," she added, holding up her index finger, "Fisheries and Oceans plotted your course and ask that you stick to it." Cathy slid a file to him. "There'll also be a helicopter on stand-by if anything goes sideways."

"I can see why they put you in charge of the Major Crime Unit, Ms. Simpson," Chuck said, giving Larry a discreet kick under the table. "And Larry told me that the commissioner wants Tony on a plate in seven days?" Chuck dipped a fry in ketchup. He immediately saw Cathy's mood change.

Cathy pushed her plate aside. "That's right. So let's make those days count."

"Get Jesse's boot and bring it back asap," Chuck pleaded.

"We'll drop it off, don't worry," Larry said.

"Oh, by the way," Chuck continued. "One of my employees, Matt, is with me now as an undercover biology student. He's staying at the King's house and hanging around to cover our bases. If you need any help, just say the word. I'll send his info and clearance to Diane."

Larry nodded, leaned back and put his arm around Cathy's chair. "We'll have cops knocking on every door in Riverside-Albert today. Keep us in the loop, Chuck."

"You bet," Chuck said as he pulled his chair away from the table.

"That Chuck," Cathy said, turning back to Larry. "Says it like it is."

"I can be more like him if you want," Larry said as he leaned closer to her in the vehicle, only a few centimetres from her smile.

Cathy crossed her legs, exposing more of her thigh. Cathy held Larry's gaze for a moment.

"What do you say we come back this way the two of us when this is all over?" she asked, smiling.

Larry laughed. "You've got yourself a deal, lady!"

CHAPTER TWENTY-EIGHT

C HUCK FOLLOWED THE BACK ROADS FROM FUNDY
Park TO Riverside-Albert on the 915 and stopped
a few kilometres past Dennis Beach. He'd hoped to
find Jesse pedalling back here. On his left, cows and horses
grazed in the fields and, on his right, the Shepody River
flowed quietly. He stepped outside for a moment, caught
in the scenery, dandelion seeds gliding delicately all around
him.

Just as Chuck was about to slip back into his vehicle,
the scenery changed. A convoy of camouflaged half-ton
army trucks spilled onto the unmarked country road. A few
trucks drove away while others pulled to the side of the road,
full-gear uniforms unloading beige-coloured quad bikes, all
kitted it seemed for serious war-zone operations. Within
minutes, the quads sped through the fields and disappeared
behind a line of spruce trees.

It all jolted him back to the reality of a killer being on
the loose. Chuck started the Explorer knowing he must find
Jesse.

Still on the 915, hairpin turns forced him to crawl at
ten kilometres an hour in some places. The straighter parts of
the road opened up to sweeping farmlands. As he approached
Riverside-Albert from the south, Chuck stopped again, this
time near Crooked Creek. From a high lookout he grabbed
his binoculars, hopelessly scanning the ribbon-shaped silver
river. He spotted two orange kayaks skimming above the
water's surface. He called Matt.

There was no sign of Jesse anywhere, Matt told him. Chuck then drove to New Ireland Road, changing to Shepody Road in the back of Fundy Park. He turned around, made his way back and parked near Midway Road in Germantown, eleven kilometres west of Riverside-Albert, hoping to see Jesse heading home on his bike. Hours later, he gave up.

Soon after receiving the 9-1-1 call, firemen and paramedics arrived at Crooked Creek and found Jesse lying unconscious near the banks. After checking for vitals, they strapped him to a spinal board and transferred him to the ambulance where they snapped on a latex tourniquet, cleaned the site, inserted an IV, hung a line and immediately started to give Jesse fluids to raise his blood pressure. Then they cranked an oxygen mask over his face. On their way to the Riverside-Albert hospital, they called it in: "Male patient, seems to be in his twenties, unconscious, a faint pulse, a patent airway and breathing. Patient is boarded with heavy bruising to upper body and face. Vitals are stable."

At the hospital, the doctor cut open Jesse's muddy T-shirt and pants and examined his body. His lacerated face was puffed up, his eyes blackened and nose crooked. Of his facial cuts, the most severe were the ones on his right eyebrow, a long one on his cheek, and one on his upper lip. He took notes of the blooming purple welts on Jesse's arms and torso and, as he poked at Jesse's injuries, Jesse came to.

Jesse yelled, "N-n-no-no!" as he tried to get up from the bed.

The doctor backed up, pulled the examination room's black leather rolling stool close to Jesse, and sat down slumping so his large frame wouldn't seem so frightening. "I'm Doctor Moore. What's your name?"

Jesse, holding his nose and quivering, said, "J-J-Jesse."

"A nurse will be here any minute to take you for x-rays. Who did this to you?"

Jesse sobbed, covered his face with his hands.

The doctor leaned in and whispered, "Are you on any medication?" Jesse nodded. "Any idea what they're called?" Jesse shook his head. "Are you from here?" Nothing. "Mind telling me where you're from?" Still no response. "As soon as your X-ray results come back, I can give you something for pain. For the time being, just hang in there, it won't be long."

The doctor scribbled down a few more notes and dropped off the file at the nurse's station. "Did we find any I.D. on this guy?"

Nurse Beverley, the only one working the ER with the doctor, looked at him like he was from another planet. "No, but I know who it is."

"Who?"

"Jesse Rawford. He's a bit slow. Lives at the Sticky Monkey. Want me to give them a call?"

"Yes, please, and page me when you're done with him."

The doctor closed the door in his office and picked up the receiver, dialing the Hillsborough Police Detachment. "We have a young man in his twenties, name Jesse Rawford, found near Crooked Creek early this morning. He took a beating."

Doctor Moore flipped on the x-ray box light and, one by one, slid the films on the illuminator plate. A broken nose and a fractured rib, he deducted. He walked back to the nurse's station. "Give him antibiotics and pain medication. Let's keep his nose nice and cold and pack his nostrils for a few days. I might be able to straighten it out once the swelling goes down. He's got a broken rib on the right-hand side. Ice pack the right side of his ribcage. And, that's not all. He's got an orbital blowout fracture, but he's conscious."

"I could tell just by the way his left eyeball sunk in," said Beverley.

"Keep a close watch on him."

Harry and his wife, Betty, arrived at the hospital at 7:30 a.m. Except for a cleaning lady emptying garbage cans along the long hallway, the hospital was quiet. As they approached the nurse's station, Beverley came out of an outpatient room.

"Hello," she said with a smile. "I've got your boy in Room 202."

"How is he?" Betty asked, deeply concerned. "What happened to him?"

Beverley guided them to Jesse's room and opened the door slightly. "He's gotten a beating. A severe eye punch, a broken nose and rib. The doctor on duty, Doctor Moore, wants to wait till the swelling goes down to fix his nose. His vision seems fine though. He's lucky, really."

"Do you know what happened?" Harry asked.

"No idea. Someone trout fishing found him along Crooked Creek."

Betty paused for a moment and shook her head. "Poor boy. Why can't they just leave him alone?"

"Is he on any medication?" the nurse asked.

Harry moved closer to the nurse and spoke quietly. "Yes. For mental illness. We give him pills every morning and every night, but I don't know what they're called. Betty?"

"I don't know either, but we could bring them in."

"Did he take them last night?" the nurse said, adjusting her eyeglasses.

"No," Betty replied. "He didn't come home last night. He does that sometimes and apparently he's always been that way."

"Since he's sleeping right now, why don't you wait a few minutes and I'll get Doctor Moore to see you. Just wait in the sitting room on your right."

That same night, the wind raced from tree to tree on King's property, making the old bat-house, hung loosely on a post, squeak. Chuck sauntered to the back door through the rock pathway and paused for a moment to watch the bats as they darted across the moonlit sky. He walked a few yards and stopped to look up at Matt standing at the upstairs' window.

Matt opened the window and put his head out. "Haven't seen him yet."

Chuck brought his index finger to his lips to silence Matt and took to the stairs two at a time. Matt was sitting in a Lazy boy chair with his feet up pointing to a paper bag on the floor. "Here's the boots you asked for."

"You have to learn to be totally undercover. And why aren't you at Harry's waiting for Jesse?"

"I've been going back and forth. I figured I might see him around."

"I told you to stay there until he comes home."

"I get it. Sorry. Want me to do the night watch?"

Chuck scratched his head, thought a moment. "No. Give me an hour. I need to tie a few loose ends here. I'll take your car and do the graveyard shift. Now, get out of here."

CHAPTER TWENTY-NINE

WHILE CATHY WAS BURIED IN PAPERWORK BEHIND her desk, Larry stood in the doorway of her office, coffee in hand.

She looked up and wiggled her fingers in a come-in motion. "Anything new? Ben?"

"Nothing. Not a peep from anyone."

"Did you check his house again?"

"Yes, twice," Larry sighed. "He's not there and no calls, in or out."

Cathy swivelled her chair to face the window. A paperweight, a hand-blown art glass, a lucky charm given by her father, sat on top a thick stack of file folders. She held it in one hand and picked up the top folder with the other hand, fanning herself. "Unbelievable," she grumbled. "Both twins are gone. What are we missing here?"

"Don't know, Cathy," Larry replied, taking a sip of his coffee. "We've combed every inch of Albert County. Unless... he's going back to where we've already been."

Cathy tossed the paperweight from hand to hand before setting the object down and, cupping her face in her hands for a moment. "Quite possible. Thankfully, the army will cover a bigger area now than we ever could."

Her office was eerily quiet. Cathy got up and pushed her hands into the small of her back, stretching her upper body backward slightly. "How did they evaporate into thin air like that? What's the latest from the command post?"

"I just went over all of the daily reports with Diane.

They've interviewed Jesse's acquaintances, mostly fishermen that he's worked for over the years. They all feel sorry for him but nobody's seen or heard anything. Unfortunately, the 1-800 tip line didn't bring any good leads. If someone saw him, they're not talking."

Larry's phone rang. "Hey," he said into the phone, walking towards Cathy's desk. "Really? *Jesse's* gone, too? No, nothing on Ben or Tony. Yes, we'll be in touch. Thanks, Chuck."

Cathy stood up. "Call the command post and get them to talk to every fisherman in Alma to find out who saw Jesse last and when."

The steam in the teapot built up and, as the vibrations grew more intense, the whistling got louder. Heather removed it from the stove and brought it to the table just as Reverend King came into the kitchen and took a bottle of homemade jam from the fridge, setting it before his guests.

Chuck pulled his chair closer to the table and nudged Matt. "Bacon and eggs. I never get tired of that."

"And the way you cook it," Matt followed. "It's to die for."

Heather brought the plates to the tables and joined them. "You getting lots done, Bob?"

"Yes, I am," he nodded while taking his first bite.

"Wish we could say the same about the manhunt," the reverend said, shaking his head. "All the police and army personnel that have gone through these parts since the manhunt started and they can't find one man. One man!"

"I see your point," Chuck said amicably. "But it's a big area."

"Naturally," Reverend King replied. "But we're sick of it. Everybody is. It's caused our schools to close for, what, six weeks now, with parents having to drive their kids to school in Moncton. It's hard when most of these people only work seasonal. This year will go down in history books as being the worst for tourism, too. No tourist will be caught in these parts."

They ate in silence for a few minutes. When they'd finished, Chuck nodded to Matt and they stood, taking their empty plates to the counter. After thanking the cook, Chuck spoke up. "Hopefully, they'll find him soon and everybody can go back to their lives."

Heather lost no time in replying, "Yes, before we all lose our marbles."

Chuck jumped in his SUV with Matt and drove to Harry's cafe, but a "Closed" sign greeted them. Chuck pulled up his jacket sleeve to check the time. "Strange that they'd be closed. Go out back and see if Jesse's bike is there."

When Matt returned and shook his head, Chuck was on the phone. He hung up and said, "Are you sure? Did you look closely?" Chuck tore away his sunglasses to study Matt's face.

"Yeah, I'm sure. Why, you don't trust me?" Matt's mouth screwed up, and Chuck knew he was chewing the inside of his cheek.

Chuck rubbed his eyes. "Shit. Sorry I snapped at you. Didn't get much sleep last night, that's all. Was talking to Diane and nobody's seen or heard from Jesse at the wharf. Let's take a drive. We'll circle back in an hour or so."

It was 7:30 a.m. An early mist was rising over Crooked Creek as Chuck wheeled onto 915, driving eight kilometres to Harvey Bank and then to Mary's Point. Cop cars were set up with roadblocks every two kilometres. On more than one occasion, Chuck spotted a handful of soldiers coming out of the woods, pulled by dogs, or kicking through fields and farmhouses. Chuck pointed to a decaying, grey barn, its rust-coloured metal roof having lost its appeal. "That'd be a good place to hide."

Matt turned his window down. "Frig, who in their right mind would hide this long?"

"Someone who doesn't want to be found, that's who," Chuck said.

On the drive back, Chuck was elated. Several cars were parked at the Sticky Monkey. A shaft of sun touched his face as he rushed to the front door, and, upon entering, smelled eggs. Harry was at the cash with a customer. "Take a seat, guys. I'll be right over."

"How you doing?" Chuck asked of Harry.

"Jesse's at the hospital," he said as he poured coffee into their cups. "Got beaten up last night near Crooked Creek."

CHAPTER THIRTY

THE HOSPITAL, A ONE-LEVEL BUILDING A LIGHT shade of blue, was hidden behind an old generation of cedars, fifteen feet high, on the edge of town. Chuck hurried up the wheelchair ramp leading to the main entrance. Once inside, the corridor was empty save for a few stuffed, cracked-vinyl chairs locked together in pairs. The linoleum shone.

Chuck found a nurse sitting at the nurse's station, her head down. She had short brown hair, navy blue attire and a stethoscope around her neck. Chuck cleared his throat and she looked up, bringing her red-rimmed eyeglasses to the tip of her nose.

"Hello," he said quietly. "I'm looking for Jesse. Jesse Rawford."

Without moving a hair, she peered at him over her glasses. "Hi. And you are?"

"I'm a friend."

She smiled kindly. "He's sleeping. I suggest you try him tonight."

"Mind if I wait by his door? I'd really like to see how he's doing."

The woman raised her right eyebrow. "Go on in for a few minutes but be quiet. He needs his rest." She rose. "Room 202."

Chuck thanked her and pushed the door gently, the hallway light spilling into the room. His gaze swivelled over the room, looking for Jesse. There he was, curled on the hospital bed, his freshly shaven head barely visible. Chuck closed the door behind him and his eyes adjusted to the light. He surveyed his surroundings – a single window, the size of a computer monitor, three empty beds, a curtain hanging limply on a chrome railing behind Jesse, and, just above Jesse's head, a panel of buttons, plugs and an ambient light.

Chuck sat patiently on a recliner beside the bed for ten minutes, trying not to make too much noise but perhaps breathing more heavily than normal. He even coughed lightly once or twice.

Jesse opened his swollen eyelids and looked at Chuck, his eyes fluttering. His eyes then grew larger. "B-B-Bob!!"

"Shhh. How you doing, buddy?"

Jesse's jaw muscles twitched. Tears streamed from his eyes.

"Who did this to you?"

Jesse's bottom lip quivered. "T-T-Tony."

Chuck slipped his hand through the side rail and touched Jesse's arm.

"Tony who?"

"M-m-my uncle T-Tony."

Chuck put his other hand in and brought a book close to Jesse's face. Jesse lifted his eyebrows and moaned from the pain. "Wh-wh-whales? M-m-mine?"

"Yes. All yours. Can you read?" Chuck asked, leaning in.

"Me c-c-c-a-a-n read," Jesse responded wryly while wrapping the book in his arms. "No-no-nobody ain't ne-ne-never g-give me a-a-a book."

"Good," Chuck said, surprised at the childlike tone of Jesse's voice. "It's yours to keep. Write your name inside the cover so nobody steals it from you. I figured you might like the pictures. When I was a kid, I wanted to be a sailor aboard a whaling ship. You know, catch them and kill them. But then I grew up and realized I liked them too much and wanted to write about them instead."

Chuck moved his chair closer and said softly, "I've heard

a lot about you from Harry and I know your life wasn't easy. Nobody deserves what you went through. I feel bad about that."

Jesse winced as he met Chuck's eyes.

"Maybe when you get out of here, I'll take you on the boat."

"Wh-wh-when?" he asked with a bright smile behind cracked lips.

"When you're feeling better. Now, tell me, what exactly do you do when you go fishing?"

"I-I-I-I b-b-bait and cl-cl-cl, clean lo-lo-lobster traps."

"And, how long have you been doing that?"

"A lo-lo-long t-t-..." Jesse murmured as he fell asleep.

Chuck returned to the nurse's station and asked the nurse how long Jesse would be in the hospital.

"Not sure, exactly," she replied. "A few days at least."

Jesse's room at Harry's had a single bed, a small chair next to it, a TV on a dresser and plenty of pill bottles on a night table. The room smelled like fresh linen hung on the line. Jesse sat up on his bed and shut off the TV as soon as Chuck walked in.

"How you holding up?" Chuck asked as he observed the bandages on Jesse's face.

"B-b-b-bored," Jesse said with a half-smile and a twisted nose.

Chuck, holding his hat, sat down and looked at Jesse who wore blue-striped pajama pants and a white T-shirt.

"B-B-B-Bob," Jesse said. "When c-c-can w-w-we g-g-go out... yo-yo-you know, on-on the boat?"

"Not for a few more days yet, Jesse. Doctor says you need to rest and heal those wounds first. I'll check with Harry and let you know ahead of time."

Jesse's face turned sad. He moved his head away from

Chuck and turned the TV back on.

"Don't worry. It won't be long."

Once in the parking lot, Chuck sat in the Explorer, hands on the wheel, his hat on the seat beside him. The plan to take Jesse out on the boat in a few days became in focus. He felt bad getting Jesse involved, but there was no other way.

Two days later, Chuck drove to the Sticky Monkey Cafe and shut his cellular off. When he raised his head, he saw Jesse in one of the windows waving to him. As soon as Chuck entered the cafe, Jesse stood in front of him, smiling from ear to ear. The bruising around Jesse's eyes was still very noticeable and the butterfly tapes were pinching the cuts on his face and head. Without a pause, Jesse flipped his drawing pad open and pulled a page out. "This fo-fo-for you, B-B-B-Bob."

It was a drawing of a whale sitting atop a high wave.

"Wow! You've really got talent. Can I use this picture for my book, you know, if I ever publish it?"

"Ye-ye-ye-yeah," Jesse said, grinning.

Chuck put his arm around Jesse's shoulder and gently guided him back to a table. "No big rush, Jesse... I need my coffee. Are you sure you're okay to head out today?"

"Yep," Jesse replied, holding on to his left side. "D-d-doctor says start b-b-biking again w-w-wh-when I feel li-li-like it."

As soon as they sat down, the doorbell rang again and Matt walked in. Chuck waved him over. "Jesse, meet Matt; Matt, meet Jesse. Matt's a student of mine. Want coffee?"

"No thanks," Matt replied as he sat next to Jesse. "It's too hot. How can you drink that shit on a hot day?"

Jesse laughed.

"Matt here can tell you what it's like to see a humpback whale breach off the starboard bow for the first time," Chuck uttered between sips of coffee. "Tell him, Matt."

Jesse smiled and said, "Me, me seen that b-b-before."

"Go figure, Bob. When are we leaving?" Matt asked impatiently.

"Leaving?" Chuck inquired as Jesse craned his head up to hear the answer. "To where, exactly?"

"I thought you and I were going out on the water today," Matt said annoyed.

"Well I promised Jesse here to take him with me," Chuck replied.

"Why can't we all go?" Matt asked, the chair legs screeching as he pushed his chair back.

"Relax, Matt," Chuck replied as he looked at Jesse. "I said I'm taking Jesse today."

"Fine," Matt replied as he rushed to the door and slammed it on his way out.

"Kids today have no manners," Chuck murmured.

"No-no-no man-man-manners," Jesse repeated, his eyes beaming.

The drive to Alma from Riverside-Albert was as spectacular as the day before. Chuck rested his elbow out the window and Jesse did the same.

"Great to be living in this part of the world, Jesse," Chuck said as he shut the radio off to avoid listening to the news. "You're only steps away from beautiful Mary's Point. Ever see the sandpipers when they come in August?"

"E-e-ever see the, the, the Rocks?" Jesse asked.

"In Hopewell Cape?" Chuck inquired, playing dumb.

"Yeah," Jesse added, stretching his neck. "They're b-b-big."

"I saw them once when I was a kid," Chuck answered. "Maybe we'll scoot over there tomorrow if we can get away from Matt," he said, which made Jesse laugh again.

"Okay," Jesse said as he squirmed in his seat with excitement.

"I brought us a lunch and a few brewskis," Chuck said. "Are you allowed to drink with your medication?"

"Yeah," Jesse replied. "I-I-I like b-b-beer!"

"Nothing like fresh air and the sound of the ocean to kick start your day, hey?"

Chuck parked next to the fishing store in front of the wharf and patted Jesse on the back as they retrieved their gear from the back of the vehicle. Jesse jumped and moved away from the vehicle.

"Sorry, Jesse, I didn't mean to hurt you," Chuck said.

Chuck noticed Jesse had turned his back to him and was pulling an old gray toque over his head. Chuck grabbed the cooler handles and carried it to the boat. "The tide is right up there today, Sketchmate. So we'll have to keep an eye on that, seeing how fast the tide drops here."

"Sk-sk-sk-sketch… mate?"

"That's your new name," Chuck shouted as he climbed down the rusty steel ladder and jumped onboard the red and black seven-meter Zodiac rescue boat – a rigid-hull inflatable equipped with a diver board, life boards and light buoys. "You sketch and you're my new mate."

After grabbing the cooler and setting it down on the boat's deck, Chuck walked over to the steering console and fired up the engine. Jesse started making his way down, but Chuck interrupted him.

"Untie us first, Sketchmate!" Chuck said. "Untie us and throw me the rope… then, take your time coming down. No rush."

Jesse threw his duffle bag in the boat and climbed down the wharf's ladder, sweaty by the time he hit the deck.

Chuck glanced at the few fishing boats still docked. Most were already offshore. A single sailboat was sitting pretty in the bay amidst a light wind and a clear sky. Above, on the wharf, a handful of kids were trying their luck at catching fish.

Once they cleared the wharf, Chuck opened the engine's throttle and turned left toward St. Martins. Along the way, they passed by leisure boats, waving at the mariners. After ten more minutes in the water, the red sea cliffs of St. Martins appeared in the distance. He turned the boat with his back to the small town and shut the engine off. With his binoculars he observed heavy, metal lobster traps breaking the surface as the fishermen winched and slid them along the washboard.

"I thought there was no fishing today..."

Jesse shrugged. "G-g-got a b-b-beer?"

"Here, Sketchmate!" Chuck handed Jesse a beer. "This okay? What kind of beer do you like?"

"Co-co-co, cold ones," Jesse said, laughing as he pulled the tab off the can. "We gonna see, see whales t-t-t-today?"

"We just might," Chuck answered, feeling bad for laying the beer on to Jesse. "But you must see all kinds of them when you're fishing, right?"

Jesse brought the beer to his mouth. "Yep."

"You're so lucky," Chuck said as he sat down. "But today what we can do is identify them. Call them by their names. Know what I mean? Didn't you bring your book? We could look them up."

Jesse unzipped his bag and pulled out the book.

"You want t-to look?" he asked.

At that same moment, Chuck noticed blood trickling from Jesse's nose and told Jesse about it. Jesse wiped his nose with his forearm. "Hold on," Chuck said as he headed to the console and pulled a few tissues from the glove box, handing them to Jesse.

"Bend forward and pinch the end of your nose."

Chuck sat back down and then flipped to the index of the book. "Here... page twenty-two; there should be a picture of a right whale." He flipped more pages. "Okay, here it is. It says that right whales are one of nature's great losers. The population that once numbered 50,000 was hunted so extensively that they were thought to be extinct. They can weigh up to a hundred tons, can you believe that? They spend half of the year feeding right here in the Bay of Fundy. This makes them vulnerable, though, because they get caught in fishing nets or wounded by boats getting too close to them."

Chuck stopped his lecture and looked at Jesse over his reading glasses, noticing the now empty beer can rolling on the boat's floor.

"Put it back in the cooler and grab another," Chuck said as he closed the book and set it on his lap. He looked at Jesse and tried to hide his guilty conscience; at this point in the investigation, he had no choice. To his right, he scanned the waters and located two boats – a fishing boat and a sailboat. Which one was listening in on their conversation?

He rubbed his chin with his index finger and thumb, making a show of it for Jesse, then leaned over and said, "Sketchmate… can I tell you a secret?"

"S-s-sure," Jesse nodded. "Wha-what?"

"Only if you swear on your mother's grave that you will never tell anyone," Chuck said, still hesitating.

Jesse shoved the bloody tissues in his duffle bag. "I-I-I swear BOB!" he replied. He pretended to zip his lips.

"Well it happened a long time ago, when I was a teenager," Chuck began as he tugged at the wind cords of his Tilley hat. "It was a full moon and a bit foggy. I decided to steal a dory and get myself some lobster. I rowed until I couldn't feel my arms anymore and I came to a buoy."

Jesse nodded, his eyes wide.

"I grabbed it," Chuck continued. "I snagged the gaff and reached over the side of the boat to pull the trap line up unto the oar's hook. I pulled at it until I was blue in the face. I should've dived in, but I couldn't swim back then."

"Then what?" Jesse asked.

"Then," he replied, pulling a piece of chewing gum out of his pocket and shoving it in his mouth, "it broke the surface and I hoisted it onto the boat. Every muscle in my body hurt, I swear. I opened the trap and tossed the smelly mackerel bait overboard. Then I grabbed half a dozen lobsters and I threw them in a pail. Are you ready for this? And, just as I was about to shut the trap and drop it back over, I heard a voice behind me."

Jesse leaned toward Chuck.

"Yeah, couldn't believe it either," Chuck said, scratching the back of his head and taking a sip of beer. "I turned around and here's this guy standing up in front of me in his dory. And then he grabs the side of my boat. He shouts, 'You rotten no-good-for-nothing thief! I'm bringing you to the cops.' That didn't sit well with me, Jesse." Chuck raised his eyebrows and Jesse returned a knowing nod. "So I unhooked one of the oars and swung it at him, hitting him across the head as hard as I could. He lost his balance and fell in the water. I never looked back."

"What-what, what happened to him?"

"He drowned that night," Chuck said with a blank face. "They fished him out later. I kept that a secret my whole life until now. And I feel bad about it. You know I didn't mean to, right?"

"Yep," Jesse said.

"You ever do anything like that?" Chuck asked.

CHAPTER THIRTY-ONE

CHUCK LOOKED THROUGH HIS BINOCULARS AGAIN and spotted a score of seagulls plunging into the waters around a lobster boat. The crew checked the traps, throwing back undersized or female lobsters with eggs. The captain banded the claws and threw the lobster in his saltwater tank.

Jesse's right leg was shaking nervously. "One day, I-I-I-I hurt a l-l-little b-b-baby."

Chuck continued to observe the fishing boat. "You didn't do it on purpose? Right?"

"NO!" Jesse cried out, clearing his voice and taking a deep breath. "T-T-Tony told me to. You, you, you're not gonna tell on m-m-me, hey?"

"Your uncle Tony? No way... Well, as long as you don't tell on me," Chuck said, trying not to interrupt too much, but he couldn't help it now that the story was rolling. "When did this happen, Sketchmate?"

Jesse said nothing, but blinked quickly.

Chuck chewed his gum and grimaced. "And where was Tony?"

"He, he was busy. T-T-Tony told me I could get a B-B-Big M-M-Mac if I did it."

"And how the heck would you stop a baby from crying? That's what I want to know."

"Put a p-p-pillow over his f-face," Jesse said with a frown. "Yeah, I-I-I did," he said flatly. "He, he, he was busy and told me t-t-to shut the baby up."

Chuck nodded and squinted at a leisure boat getting closer.

"Did Tony hurt the rest of that family?"

Jesse nodded and downed another beer.

"Did Tony keep his promise?"

"N-n-no, not yet..."

"What about Ben? You must know him."

"Yep. He, he, he's m-m-my un-uncle too. He, he's got p-p-p-pretty girls," he said, giggling.

"Do you have any weapons?"

Jesse looked at Chuck blankly, then shrugged and unzipped his duffle bag and sifted through its contents. Chuck felt a chill go far down his spine.

"A knife. N-n-no gun," Jesse said, showing him a five-inch palette knife, a one-piece tempered steel blade used for art. Jesse held it up in the air on display."

Chuck finished his beer and put the can back in the cooler, while nodding to the speed boat. Jesse turned around and noticed the craft approaching. He shoved the palette knife back in his bag, shoved the toque further down his head and took a slurp of his beer.

"Wha-wha-what d-d-do they want?" Jesse asked, his face turning pale as he scratched his cheek.

"No idea," Chuck replied, his back to Jesse. "Probably tourists with no idea where the heck they're going."

Chuck walked towards the stern and waved at Wilbur Mitcham who was now standing no more than twenty feet away.

"Is that you, Bob?" Wilbur asked as he tilted his sunglasses on his forehead to get a better look at the skipper. "Well, I'll be damned! I should have known you'd be kicking around here whale-watching."

"Damn straight," Chuck shouted.

"Mind if we join you guys? My wife here stopped at the liquor store, got herself some coolers but didn't think to buy me beer."

"Sorry, Wilbur. We're in kind of a hurry. Got to head

back. How about I call you one of these days instead?"

"Please do," Mitcham said. He then waved and steered the boat away.

Chuck looked back and saw the tension and worry slip from Jesse's face.

Night ate away at daylight and slivers of shadow began to fall around Ben as he sped down the last ten-kilometre strip of Niagara Road, the only light his high beams stabbing the road's shoulders. His mind wandered and the blackness brought up hatred. He wished that he was far away, behind the controls of his monoplane or that he could at least drag the sun back out. He met a car flashing its headlights. Was it a cop or were his high beams on? Ben quickly switched his headlights back to low-beam. Seeing a cop right now would be a blessing.

Tony ducked down and Ben's headlights caught a pair of eyes through the trees. They disappeared as quickly as they appeared. Deer, most likely. Tony pulled himself back up into the seat and spoke, "Slow down. It's around here."

Ben clinched the steering wheel and pulled the Jeep into a hidden driveway. His mind raced and he broke into a cold sweat.

"Kill the lights," Tony demanded. "Go slow and park behind the building."

"What building? I don't see a building."

"Go straight. You'll see it soon enough. It's overgrown with bush."

"Is this even a road?"

"Oh, for God's sake, quit your whining."

After about two hundred feet in, Tony told Ben to steer right and the building loomed out of the blackness. Ben parked behind the structure and Tony ordered him out, turning on the headlight mounted on his forehead. Tony then pulled a flashlight out of his cargo pants, the beam shining through overgrown cedars, withering apple trees and older staghorn sumacs around the property. In the shadows, Ben made out the shape of a rusted bulldozer lying on its side against a high chain-link fence.

Ben's senses were heightened. In the distance, over the sound of leaves crunching under his feet, he heard the screech of an owl.

Tony shoved at Ben's back. "Move it."

"What's gotten into you?" Ben snapped back through gritted teeth as he walked over loose chunks of slate on the overgrown pathway.

"Quiet," Tony hissed.

The backdoor squealed and banged in the wind. Ben's skin crawled at the sight of the derelict building. There were only shards of glass in the windows and when they reached the back entrance, the cement steps were crumbling and broken.

Tony rattled the loose door handle and flakes of rusted paint fell to the ground. Ben hesitated. The same feeling of dread that had kept him awake as a child settled in. He tried to take a deep breath but only small gasps of air got in or out.

He pulled himself together and walked inside. Tony's flashlight revealed a floor trashed with empty beer bottles, ceiling plaster and animal debris. In the first room, the wind whistled through a shattered window. The peeling wallpaper hung limp in what could have been a kitchen; its counter was covered in thick grey dust. Ben tried to control his breathing as their footsteps echoed on the floorboards. Two wooden support beams stood guard in the adjoining room, barely holding the sagging ceiling. The walls' exposed slats gave it a gaunt look.

"This Parker's old mill?" Ben asked, trying to kill the tension in the room.

"Yep," Tony said. "He knew people had no other job to go to and treated them like shit."

A look of disgust came over Ben's face and, stuffing his hands in his pockets, he turned around and balked in defiance, his feet locked to the floor.

"Smells like somebody died in here." He paused. "What do you want with me?"

Tony pointed the flashlight's beam at Ben's face. "Somebody probably did!"

Ben raised his voice this time. "What the hell are we doing here, Tony?"

"Oh, shut up!" Tony shouted with frustration as he pushed Ben deeper in.

They entered an oversized room, empty save for the carcass of a filing cabinet. On the back wall, Tony's flashlight revealed a wooden door. Tony moved slightly ahead of Ben and opened it, its joints creaking.

Ben backed up slowly.

"Get in!"

Ben gulped and passed through, wrestling with the cobwebs. "This your hiding place?"

"You'll see soon enough."

Once inside, a musty smell settled in his nose and he heard a noise. A rustle made him freeze. At that moment, Tony grabbed the back of his shirt. With his free hand, he shed light on the small, dark room. Ben followed the beam of light to the far wall.

"Here's your pretty lady," Tony said, laughing as he let go of him.

Ben locked eyes with Maryel and, for an extended second, he stood motionless. Tied and gagged, Maryel was sitting on a filthy mattress, her back against concrete. Her eyes screamed fear. Ben choked back his anger, his legs barely holding him up.

"And I'm an uncle," Tony blurted out as he moved the beam of light to another wall.

Alec, also tied, lay wide-eyed on the floor. Ben ran to Maryel and then to Alec.

"You bastard! Have you lost your mind?"

"Something like that."

"There are cops all around here!" Ben shouted, his eyes

trying to reason with him. "You trying to get us all killed?"

"Cops have been here already and gone. I was right behind them every step of the way."

Ben stood up inches from Tony. "What do you want?"

Tony widened his stance. "I have a grand plan."

"Did you blow up the pub and the camp?" Ben asked, crossing his arms. Tony stared at Ben. "Didn't you want to get rid of them?"

"What about Ken and his wife?"

"Payback, brother. Bastard hit me when I was a kid."

"So, you kill his wife too...and Tina? What did she ever do to you?"

"She didn't want to talk to me... said I reminded her too much of Dad. I'm *nothing* like Dad."

Tony tossed the flashlight to the ground, knocking the light out of it, and turned out of the room. Ben scrabbled at the floor to find it. Thank God, he thought, shaking it back to life. Holding it between his teeth, he freed Maryel and Alec. She shivered and Alec looked confused. He wanted to cover them with a blanket, wash the tears off her cheeks and bring her piercing blue eyes back.

"I thought he was going to kill us," she sobbed, confused.

They were holding on to each other when Tony returned, grinning and rubbing his hands in mock glee. "Well, well, well... a family reunion. Ain't that just sweet? Now say goodbye to them."

"Goodbye?" Ben stammered.

"This is the only way out, *brother*. I have the whole place wired, the *whole* place, and we're all going to be blown to glorious pieces. I'm doing you a favour. You think I'm crazy? I'm the good guy here. And they just can't get off my back. Why can't they just get off my freakin' back? They don't get it. They think they'll catch me but they'll never catch *me*. No way. Not me."

Tapping at his chest, spit coming out of his mouth, Tony's voice raised. "You know I made it this far without anybody's help... I mean *nobody*. All I was ever good at, and I mean *really* good at, was killing people. So it's only fair that I end it the same way. And there's nothing they can do about it. We all had a shitty life, Ben. Look at Alec. Do you think he gives a damn? He's better off dead. All of us are better off dead."

Speaking fast and trying not to break down, Ben moved slowly towards Tony. "Why don't we run like hell and move out of this hole once and for all? I can set up shop anywhere you want to live. I'll take care of you and Maryel's got a good job, too. You'll never have to worry about a thing."

Tony paced. "I, I, I... always about *you*, Ben." He swore, then wiped the spittle from his face with the back of his hand. "You have no idea what I've done in my life. If you did, you wouldn't be trying to convince me of anything." Tony paused and looked down as though remorseful.

The room seemed to be closing in on Ben. The flashlight's beam flickered and Ben tried to stop his voice from shaking. "I don't care what you've done, Tony. You're my brother. Let's get out of here and figure it out together like we did back at the motel."

Tony shrugged and stared off into space with a dreadful look. "We're not starting anything, Ben. Can't you see the whole world is against us? It's been since the day we were born. We're not starting anything, you hear me? This is the end and there's nothing you can do. It's all set. The place will be..." he paused, as if searching for the perfect word, "*obliterated* in minutes."

Ben turned to Maryel, closed his eyes for a split of a second and tried to take a deep breath. His nerves bounced in his gut. Maryel put her head on his chest and, with a plaintive voice, whispered, "I love you."

Ben opened Maryel's hand and slapped the flashlight in it before letting go.

Before Tony could react, Ben flew at him in a football tackle. They both fell to the floor and Tony, clothing tearing, got out of Ben's grip. Tony sprang up and a foot came down on Ben's face, pinning him. Ben grabbed Tony's leg and pried away at it long enough to wiggle his head out and bite the ankle bone. Tony cursed and stepped back. When Ben got to his feet, Tony connected the first punch.

Ben staggered, used Tony's headlamp as a target and punched back hard. Tony's cheek split open and he stumbled. Ben kept punching. At last, Tony fell and blacked out for a few seconds. Ben unbuckled his belt and tried to wrap it around Tony's neck. Tony slipped the tip of his finger under but Ben pulled tighter, looped the belt in its buckle again and pulled at one end of the strap as though in a tug-of-war.

"Go to hell, Ben," Tony grunted, gulping for air.

Ben straightened his arms and locked them in, bent one knee, and pushed on Tony's shoulder with his foot.

He pulled on the belt with all of his might. Tony fought back, his legs jerking, kicking at the floor. Thick droplets of blood dribbled down Ben's mouth. If only he had a gun. He kept pulling until Tony went limp.

He let go and reached for Maryel to give him the flashlight. She stood against the wall, holding a shaking Alec. Her cri de coeur "Ben!" prompted him to turn. Tony, still on the floor, stabbed Ben in the leg.

Ben roared and grabbed Tony's wrist, pulling the hand with the slippery hunting knife from his lower thigh. Blood gushed, but Ben ignored the pain. He fell on his brother, stabbing him in the chest, bones cracking and blood spurting out from the wound. "God damn you, God damn you," he cried until Tony's head slumped and his body stopped thrashing. For a second, Ben stared at Tony's lifeless body.

A jolt hit Ben and he grabbed the flashlight, picked up Alec, then he and Maryel jumped out the nearest window.

"Run, babe," Ben shouted as he limped, holding on to Alec. "Run as hard as you can."

CHAPTER THIRTY-TWO

L ARRY COULDN'T SLEEP, COULDN'T HELP BUT THINK about Cathy. He tossed and turned and finally gave up, switching the television on and watching *The National*. Just like every other night, the fugitive was on the set. The wording changed a bit, and tonight the media was interviewing Alma residents as they went about their business. He took a deep breath and cracked his knuckles.

He was trying to relax when his pager buzzed. He brought the hotel phone's receiver to his ear and dialled the number.

"Detective White?" The voice on the other end echoed slightly.

"Yes."

"Ben Walsh called here looking for you."

"Really? Are you sure?"

"Yes," the officer continued. "He left a number. Says it's urgent."

Larry jotted the number down and dialled it the moment the officer hung up.

"Ben," Larry said as the phone picked up on the first ring.

"What a freakin' nightmare, Larry."

"What's going on?"

"Tony. He forced me to go to an old mill... where he had my wife and kid tied up... He had the place wired and I had no choice. I killed him to get us out. He'd gone completely mad! God."

"Wait. He's dead? Where... where's his body?"

"In the burning mill. He had it wired, like I said. It was self-defense, Larry. I swear."

"Where are you, Ben?"

"On Niagara Road."

"Which side of Niagara?"

"Pine Glen side. About a mile in."

Stay put," he said. "I'm on my way."

Larry called Cathy before heading out of town. Fifteen minutes later Larry found Ben, Maryel and Alec huddled together on the side of the road, the fire ablaze in the woods behind them. Ben was shirtless and his upper thigh was wrapped. His face was a mess and Maryel was as pale as wax. Larry grabbed a blanket from the trunk and wrapped it around Maryel and Alec.

"First responders are on their way," Larry said. Before long sirens blared and lights flashed into the night. Larry asked Maryel to stay with Alec in the back seat until everything was sorted out. Maryel refused, moved closer to Ben.

"He needs his leg looked at," Larry said, voice full of understanding. "Paramedics will patch him up and then, you and I, we'll take him to the hospital." Maryel nodded and settled in the back seat with Alec. Larry then signalled one of the arriving officers to stay with them.

Larry escorted a limping Ben to the ambulance, then scanned the road for Cathy. Firefighters had reached the scene and were stretching their lines. Larry spotted Cathy running to the platoon chief. He hurried to her.

As he got closer, he heard her yell over the noise. "We have reasons to believe that the body of Tony Walsh is in there!" She flung a hand towards the fire.

"In the northwest corner from what I'm told," Larry added.

"Please, hurry and get him out now. I don't have to tell you how important this is."

"Yes ma'am," the fireman replied. "We're on it."

Cathy turned to Larry. "Where's Ben?"

"Getting checked by paramedics. Leg wound. His wife and kid are in my car. I'll want to take them to the hospital myself."

"Why would you do that?"

"Because he's been through hell and doesn't trust anybody."

Cathy lifted her chin up and he could see the muscle clenching along her jaw line. "You can't do that. We need to interrogate him."

"I'll do the interrogation. Trust me. I'm wired. Give me a few hours with him at the hospital. You know what I can do."

"All you have is two hours, tops."

Cathy picked up her phone and dialled. "Diane. Get Dr. Watson down to the morgue now and then call Robert Patterson at the command post for Tony's dental records. I know they have them. They need to be sent to the morgue. Meet me there."

Within ten minutes the firefighters had the blaze under control, and after extinguishing the flames they brought a deceased male in a body bag. Cathy moved close to the firemen holding the bag.

"Can you put him down for a minute and unzip the bag, please?"

Cathy and Diane fought through the media outside the Moncton Hospital and took the elevator downstairs. Machinery whined. As soon as the elevator doors slid open, they hurried to the morgue door and rang the bell. Dr. Gail Patrick opened the door wearing a plastic apron, rubber boots and a wide grin. Beethoven's Symphony No. 5 was cranked up.

Karen made a come-on-in motion and then walked to the stereo and killed the music. "Nice to see you guys again," she said as she snapped on her latex gloves. Lifting a finger in the air, she added, with a mischievous look on her face, "By the way, your commissioner and puppets haven't stopped calling. I told him that the body we have is in fact *very* dead and that he would be notified as soon as the results are confirmed. Damn hard to do my job when they keep interrupting."

Cathy and Diane followed her to an aluminum table with raised edges, faucets and drains. Karen unfolded the white sheet down to the dead body's waist. A partially charred torso was sitting on a rubber block, which extended the upper chest's arch. The face was intact and the corpse's glassy eyes were fixed blindly on the ceiling. The room smelled of fire.

"You've been busy," Cathy noted.

"I just happened to be here tonight with a few attendants. Lucky break for you, I guess. I have a lot of work yet to do, but what you want is an I.D."

Diane stepped closer to the table. "Are those stab wounds on his chest?"

Karen walked over to a counter and picked up a saw and, returning to them, said, "I call that penetrating trauma to the chest. You call them stab wounds to the heart." She paused, then carolled, "Tomayto, tomahto."

Cathy leaned in, close to the head. "The resemblance to Ben is incredible." Turning toward Karen, Cathy said, "Don't want to waste your time, but can you give us a ball park as to how long?"

"That's up to Doctor Bryan O'Toole, our odontologist. He's already taken x-rays, exposed the jaws surgically and is comparing his findings to the deceased's dental records as we speak. We should have the results within the hour."

❄

At noon, Larry was out of the shower and dressed in his RCMP uniform, flicking a speck of white fuzz from one of the sleeves. He looked in the mirror, pulling his red serge tunic, his yellow striped midnight blue breeches tucked into his high-brown leather riding boots. He brushed one or two falling lines of grey hairs from the shoulders of his jacket, adjusting the brown leather belt around his waist before stepping outside.

His phone rang and he picked up. "On my way, Cathy. Meet you there."

Camera operators showed up early and one by one they set the video cameras on tripods and screwed lenses into cameras, aiming their spyglasses to the podium in front of the room. A dozen or so reporters, on edge, were seated in the press conference room.

Cathy arrived at the RCMP detachment in a navy blue uniform, brass badges flashing from every direction. Clutching a black notebook in her hand, she came out gingerly from the sideline and walked up to the podium in front of a dozen microphones, a drooping, motionless, red and white flag on a pole to her left. She surveyed the crowd.

Larry, his stomach growling, stood in attention at the right-hand side of the stage.

"Good afternoon," Cathy said, looking up. "I'm Catherine d'Entremont-Simpson, Head of the Special Crime Unit in Atlantic Canada here in Moncton, New Brunswick, and the Commanding Officer of the Joint Task Force assembled to find Tony Walsh. As you know, this massive manhunt has been unfolding for exactly fifty days now and I'm here today to provide a statement in regard to Tony Walsh." She paused, glanced up briefly, then returned to her script. "On Wednesday, April seventeenth, at approximately 10:35 p.m., we received a call relating to a fire on Niagara Road in Lower Coverdale, just south of Riverview. First responders and our Special Crimes Unit were called to the scene and subsequently found a body inside an abandoned wood mill, which was on fire. As of this morning, we were able to officially identify that body as Tony Walsh of Tower Woods Road north of Marysville, New Brunswick." The crowd hushed and she checked her notes one last time. "Although the investigation is still ongoing, we are confident that the manhunt is over. At this point, this is all of the information I have. As more information becomes available, you will certainly be updated."

CHAPTER THIRTY-THREE

As Chuck sat behind the wheel of his Ford Explorer, driving down to Fundy Park, he related a cherished memory, telling Christine about him and Jesse, how they'd searched a vacant realty lot weeks earlier looking for the Graveyard Freak and how he'd grown fond of him.

It was Friday evening, the long weekend of July, and Christine said nothing, just listened, content that they were both retired now and that Chuck was willing to share the story of a young man with her.

In the middle of a sentence, and while passing a convenience store on the quiet 114, something caught Chuck's eye. He turned around and parked next to a bicycle at the store.

After a few minutes, Jesse strolled out of the store with a blue raspberry Slurpee in one hand. He moved his bike with his free hand to the back of the store and set his eyes on Shepody Marsh's pastures and farmland down below. Chuck jumped out of the vehicle and walked towards him. A sudden breeze stirred about and the wooden sign hanging under the store's eve squeaked. Life stood still for a moment as Chuck took in a breath, fingered the brim of his Tilley hat and observed Jesse. He noticed the tan on him and how his black hair had grown back, how he wore frayed, cut-off jeans, a black Harley Davidson tank top and rubber boots.

When Jesse saw Chuck, he waved his free hand excitedly in the air and broke into a big grin. Chuck noticed that the scars on Jesse's face and head had faded.

"Long time no see," Chuck said, grinning.

"Yo-yo, mo-moved."

"I did. Got me another job. You still living at Harry's?"

Jesse tightened the grip on his handle bar and raised his chin, aiming his drink at Chuck's vehicle. "Wh-who's that?"

"My sister, and I have to take her home," Chuck said as he got closer to Jesse and squeezed his shoulder. "Sure was nice seeing you, Jesse. You take care."

Jesse slurped the rest of his drink, wiped his lips with the back of his hand and threw the empty drink in a garbage can. "B-bye, B-B-Bob."

Dawn shrunk into daylight and flowers unlocked under the sunny, hot July day. Cathy closed her eyes and listened to the sound of the tide, the calls of shorebirds and chatter of squirrels as they jumped from one tree branch to another. On the cool, crisp air the sweet aroma of honeysuckle made its way to her nostrils. She sat up in a lotus yoga pose, bringing her hands to her shoulders and then all the way up, stretching her upper body.

She fixed her hair in a high ponytail before stepping outside the tent wearing shorts and a tank top. Two ring-neck pheasants, a male and a female, walked gracefully within twenty meters of her, chicks in tow. She blinked and froze, making sure not to disturb their morning stroll. Larry, sitting on a folding lawn chair nearby, grinned as he sipped his coffee from a granite-ware tin cup. Once she stopped admiring her feathered neighbours, she looked over in awe at the Village of Alma below. The warmth of the sun permeated her bare skin.

"The population really swells up here in the summer," Larry said without looking at her. "It's like a beehive down there."

"Sure is."

"Couldn't you live out here during the summer?"

"Only if I get running water," she answered, absentmindedly knotting a lock of her hair on her finger.

Larry stood and pulled her against him. "I'm so glad you accepted my offer." He then guided her mouth to his and nibbled on her bottom lip. She intercepted, returning with a passionate kiss.

"Tell me," he whispered in her ear while splaying and running his hand through the pony tail. "Will there be more camping like this for us?"

"I hope so," she replied. "As long as you promise to do all of the work while I go for a run."

"I'm really falling for you in case you haven't noticed."

She smiled.

"Hey lovebirds," Chuck said as he walked towards them holding Sharon's hand and a few fishing rods. "Great to be alive on such a fine morning, isn't it?"

"I had a ball sitting around the campfire with you guys last night," Sharon said, bending down to rub some fly dope on her bare legs. "It was a first for me. Roasting marshmallows."

"Oh yeah," Larry said, jumping up and then opening the propane stove on the picnic table. "I did promise you guys breakfast."

Chuck rubbed his belly comically. "Yeah, you did. And I'm starving."

"Who knew," Cathy said, "that we'd be all here, together, having fun. I mean, just months ago..."

"And whatever happened to the goalie mask?" Chuck chimed as he reached for the coffee pot. "Ever find it?"

Cathy grabbed the handle first. "Here, let me get you some. Sharon?"

"Yes, by all means," she replied, pointing a finger at Chuck. "He's a snorer."

"No," Larry replied, winking at Chuck. "Never found it but I did talk to Ben a few weeks ago. Was really happy to have his wife and kid back and, would you believe it, Tony had life insurance for half a million which..." he shook his head... "he left to Ben."

Chuck's brow wrinkled. "Bizarre, but Ben deserves it. He's a good kid, and he'll turn his life around now that he's clear of all that garbage."

Still with coffee pot in hand, Cathy said, "And thanks to your cock-and-bull story about killing someone while stealing lobster, which was very entertaining I may add, we were able to close that case for good. The last I heard, Jesse was hospitalized for thirty days of observation, then found not criminally responsible for killing the baby on account of his mental disorder. Which makes sense. The judge, prosecutors and defense attorneys all agreed that he just doesn't have the mental capacity to understand that what he did to that baby was wrong. And add Tony's threats, the beating afterward... He was released but will have to go before the review board annually to make sure he doesn't pose a threat to the public."

"Which reminds me," Chuck said. "We saw Jesse on the way here last night. He hasn't changed a bit. Rubber boots and all, riding his bike from Fundy to Riverside-Albert."

CHAPTER THIRTY-FOUR

S HE FOUND HERSELF IN A STAIRCASE, EACH STEP disappearing behind her as she moved to the next. She had a choice: keep going or jump. She chose the latter, leaped and fell down a long tunnel, her body sliding fast. She couldn't grip the surface. She wanted claws, claws to stop her fall, to climb back where she came from, but no, she didn't want to go there again. Her fall gained more speed. She fell to the centre of the earth, to an inferno – the heat unbearable. She paddled back through the tube, this time she had an oar and the tunnel had water. But she lost the oar and the boat. It was useless. A skinny figure, at least seven feet tall, appeared, his head twice the size it should be. An alien, maybe. Yes, definitely an alien. He is an alien. He wants to talk to her, to explain everything. She's not interested. He's ugly. He slaps her across the head, her body crumples to the dirt.

"Ben!"

Ben switched on the night table's light and hugged a sweating Maryel. He curled her up in his arms like a child. Bear, excited by the commotion, jumped on top of them.

"On the floor, Bear. Now. Oh, sweetheart. You had a bad dream."

"Was I yelling? Did I wake you?"

"No... shhhhh. I was already awake. You had a nightmare."

Ben closed his eyes and thought about how, more and more and for longer periods of time, he was happier than he'd ever been. They were slowly getting back to normal and having a life again. A life when a simple cup of coffee and watching Alec was all that he needed. He still dealt with bouts of anger and anxiety, but he had cleaned the house inside out, thrown out all of the carpets, the rugs and every last residue of the gang's intrusion in his life. All the demons were gone now, even the mask was buried in the back yard.

The night now quiet, he held Maryel, thinking she was asleep. Then, quietly, she said, "I have a doctor's appointment tomorrow."

Ben's heart skipped a beat. "For what?"

"I haven't had my period for two months."

He reached over and turned her on her back. He studied her face. Her eyes widened and she gave him a romantic gaze.

"That is awesome."

"You sure?"

"Of course. I'm positive."

He switched off the light and closed his eyes, contemplating the tenderness of her belly against his hand. He heaved a joyous sigh of relief.

Acknowledgements

Writing a book is as much about writing as it is about having the knowledge and support of many. I want to thank:

My HUSBAND, who read earlier drafts and put up with me. I'm forever indebted to him for showing me love and patience instead of strangling me and throwing the book in the shredder.

ANGELLA CORMIER for being such a great friend, a beta-reader extraordinaire and also designing the best cover I could ever imagine.

MARJORIE MOORE for reading the book along the way and providing her kind words that helped me get through the snow blizzards.

KEZIA WILLIAMSON for letting me take over her life for a while and convincing her friend Vicky Doucette to jump in. Both have been instrumental in lending this book the much-needed legal and police-investigation expertise it needed.

The YW WRITES STRONG SISTERHOOD group (who could take over the world) for allowing me to read parts of my book to them and not kicking me out.

And last, but not least, LEE THOMPSON for his relentless editorial guidance, keen insight and ongoing support in making this story come to life.

Monique Thébeau is an English-to-French translator by trade who has always preferred escaping the boundaries of business, technical and legal writing to learn more about the English language, often while exploring the limitless, dreamlike world of fiction, especially in mysteries and thrillers. Begun with a few scribbled notes ten years ago, *In the Dark of Winter* is her debut novel. Monique currently lives in Riverview, New Brunswick, Canada.

www.ingramcontent.com/pod-product-compliance
Lightning Source LLC
Chambersburg PA
CBHW071329250626
47159CB00004B/1520